project SWeet Life

Also by

BRENT HARTINGER

Split Screen

Grand & Humble

The Order of the Poison Oak

The Last Chance Texaco

Geography Club

BRENT HARTINGER

project Sweet Life

HARPER TEEN

An Imprint of HarperCollinsPublishers

HarperTeen is an imprint of HarperCollins Publishers.

Project Sweet Life
Copyright © 2009 by Brent Hartinger
Map copyright © 2009 by HarperCollins Publishers
All rights reserved. Printed in the United States of America. No part of this book may be used or reproduced in any manner whatsoever without written permission except in the case of brief quotations embodied in critical articles and reviews. For information address HarperCollins Children's Books, a division of HarperCollins Publishers, 10 East 53rd Street, New York, NY 10022.

www.harperteen.com

Library of Congress Cataloging-in-Publication Data
Hartinger, Brent.
    Project Sweet Life / Brent Hartinger. — 1st ed.
        p.   cm.
    Summary: When their fathers insist that they get summer jobs, three fifteen-year-old friends in Tacoma, Washington, dedicate their summer vacation to fooling their parents into thinking that they are working, which proves to be even harder than having real jobs would have been.
    ISBN 978-0-06-082411-2 (trade bdg.)
    [1. Moneymaking projects—Fiction.   2. Summer employment—Fiction.   3. Friendship—Fiction.   4. Tacoma (Wash.)—Fiction.]   I. Title.
PZ7.H2635Pr 2009   2008019644
[Fic]—dc22   CIP
                                                                        AC

Typography by Joel Tippie
10 11 12 13   CG/RRDB   10 9 8 7 6 5 4 3
❖

First Edition

For Michael Jensen

For making my own life very sweet indeed

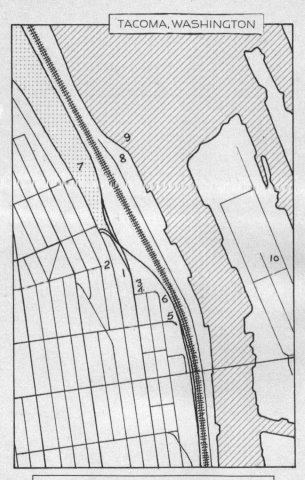

TACOMA, WASHINGTON

1. Old City Hall
2. Spanish Steps
3. Meconi's Pub
4. Olympus Hotel
5. Totem Pole
6. Fireman's Park
7. Greenbelt
8. Thea Foss Park
9. Dive Site
10. Tideflats

WEEK 1:

The Idea

"Dave," my dad said at dinner, "it's time you got yourself a summer job."

"What?" I said. The only reason I didn't choke on my spaghetti meat loaf is because he couldn't have said what I'd thought he said. True, it was the night before the first day of summer vacation. But I was only fifteen years old. For most kids, fifteen is the year of the optional summer job: You *can* get one if you really want one, but it isn't *required*. And I really, really didn't want one.

My dad is a real man's man, a straight-backed guy with a buzz cut and a deep rumble of a voice. For him, things are always very black-and-white.

"It's definitely time you got a job," he repeated, gnawing on the meat loaf like a grizzly bear. "Get out in the world, meet some up-and-comers. After all, you are who you surround yourself with." This last part was something my dad was always saying—something about birds of a feather and all that.

But even now I didn't choke on my food, because I was still certain he was kidding about my getting a job. Even if in the weirdest reaches of some wild, alternate universe where my father suddenly *did* think I should get a job the summer of my fifteenth year, even *he* wasn't so cruel as to bring it up on the night before the start of my vacation.

"Yeah, right," I said, taking another bite. "How about superspy? Between shadowing drug runners in South American nightclubs and cracking safes in Monaco casinos, I'll still be able to sleep in."

My dad sighed. "Dave, Dave, Dave," he said. This was his standard expression of disappointment in me. "It's high time you stop relying on your mother and me for money. This is the summer you start paying your own way in life. No more allowance for you. This is the summer you get a job."

Now I choked on my spaghetti meat loaf! Not only was my dad forcing me to get a summer job, he was also stopping my allowance?

"But, Dad!" I said. "I'm only fifteen!"

"What does that have to do with anything?" he said.

I tried to explain how fifteen was the summer of the optional summer job.

"Says who?" my dad said.

"Says everyone!" I said. "That's just the way it works! It's probably in the Bible somewhere. Or maybe the U.S. Constitution."

"I don't think so."

I looked at my mom, but she was blankly sipping her raspberry-mango juice blend. It was clear I wasn't going to get any help from her.

"Well, it *should* be," I said.

My dad just kept wolfing down the spaghetti meat loaf.

Before I go too far on this, I need to explain how I feel about work in general and summer jobs in particular. I don't want anyone thinking I am some sort of anti-American or anti-work deadbeat.

I believe in work. Without it, civilization collapses: Buildings don't get built, pipes stay clogged, breath mints would go unstocked. Personally, I *like* it when I use the public restroom and find that the toilet paper dispenser has been refilled.

I also believe in the idea that the harder you work, the more you should get paid. You're too tired to work? Well, then I guess you're also too tired to eat.

Work is important. I get that.

That said, I *do* work. Hard. At school, for ten months every year. Unlike a lot of people my age, I take school very seriously. My eighth-grade report on Bolivia was as comprehensive as anything in *The New York Times Almanac*. One of my freshman English essays was almost *frighteningly* insightful into the significance of those worn steps at the school in *A Separate Peace*.

And, yes, I certainly understand that some people, even some fifteen-year-olds, *need* to work. They're saving for college, or they have to help pay bills around the house. For them, a summer job at fifteen isn't optional. But my dad makes a good living as a land surveyor. He wears silk ties! And my mom is stay-at-home. We aren't poor.

The adults won't tell you this, but I absolutely knew it in my bones to be true: Once you take that first summer job, once you start working, you're then expected to *keep* working. For the rest of your life! Once you start, you can't stop, ever—not until you retire or you die.

Sure, I knew I'd have to take a job next summer. But now, I had two uninterrupted months of absolute freedom ahead of me—two summer months of living life completely on my own terms. I knew they were probably my last two months of freedom for the next fifty years.

The point is, dad or no dad, I was going to be taking a job the summer of my fifteenth year over my dead body.

"My dad is making me get a summer job," said my best friend Victor Medina later that night. "*And* he's stopping my allowance."

"You're *kidding!*" said my other best friend, Curtis Snow. "So is mine!"

We'd met in the old bomb shelter in Curtis's backyard after dinner. The shelter had been dug in the early 1960s but had been abandoned until Curtis had talked his parents into letting him, Victor, and me turn it into our own personal hideaway. And what a hideaway! We'd brought in carpet, a really plush couch, and these giant oversize floor pillows. We'd also wired in electricity from the house, which let us add things like a little refrigerator, a movie-style popcorn popper, even a flat-screen television and game system—all top-notch stuff that we'd picked up at bargain prices at garage sales and on eBay. Even Curtis's parents didn't know about everything we had hoarded in there, mostly because we'd long since installed a thick lock on the door, designed to be so secure that it would even keep out panicky neighbors clawing to get inside after the launch of a nuclear missile, and no one knew the combination except us.

"Wait," I said. "This is too weird. My dad is making *me* get a summer job too."

We stared at one another, trying to make sense of this amazing coincidence. The air smelled like raspberry syrup from our Sno-Kone machine.

Curtis, Victor, and I have been friends for years. Curtis is the Big Picture Guy, outgoing and impulsive, a great talker and an even better liar. He likes stories of all kinds, and life is never dull when he's around. He's blond, athletic, and pretty good-looking, with rosy cheeks and tousled hair. But his looks are deceptive, like those tropical clown fish that are bright and colorful and innocent-looking but which really exist just to lure other fish into the poisonous tentacles of a sea anemone. Still, the fact that Curtis looks like a choirboy is why people don't strangle him for lying, which he usually shrugs off as "shading the truth." On the downside, well, along with the lies, he talks a lot.

Victor is the opposite of Curtis. He isn't blond or athletic. He's a small guy, Hispanic, with glasses. He's well-groomed and combs his hair in an eerily even part. I sometimes think of him as a character in some black-and-white movie—not the lead but the sarcastic best friend who mumbles witty asides in the background. Victor is more practical than Curtis, and more detail-oriented, which may be why he likes science and computers. He's a watcher, not a doer. On the downside, he can be prickly and panics easily.

As for me, Dave, I am kind of like a mix between Victor and Curtis, and not just because I have a medium build and brown hair with an uneven part. It's the way

I act, too, always torn between dreaming big and being cautious. What's my downside? I don't really think I have one. Then again, I don't have to be friends with me.

But if Curtis, Victor, and I were different in some ways, we were all in complete agreement when it came to summer jobs for fifteen-year-olds.

"Our dads talked," Victor said. "It's the only explanation. Saint Craptilicus," he added with a mutter. Victor's family is old-school Catholic. He says that since there are already so many saints in the church, it doesn't matter if he adds a few more. So now, whenever the situation calls for it, he invokes new, custom-made saints.

He was also right about our dads. They work together at the county surveyors' office; their being friends is how the three of us met in the first place. They eat lunch together, go out for beer and darts after work every Tuesday, and sometimes play golf on the weekends too. It couldn't be a coincidence that all three had suddenly decided their sons needed to get summer jobs. It had probably happened on the golf course that very afternoon.

"I wonder whose idea it was," I said.

"My dad," Curtis said.

"My dad," Victor said.

I, of course, was positive it was *my* dad who had brought it up. I could almost hear the conversation:

You know, Ray, ever notice how easy *our sons have it?*

They sure do, Brian! A lot easier than we had it when we *were their age! Don't they, Andy?*

Absolutely right! And it's high time they pull their own weight!

Build some character!

Learn the way the world really *works!*

"First they say we're just kids," Victor said. "That we can't surf the internet without filters or buy this video game or go to that movie. But then they want to make us take on all the responsibilities of an adult? They can't give us the responsibilities without the privileges! That's not fair."

"Amen!" Curtis said. "Sing it, brother! I mean, if being a kid means anything at all, it means summer vacation. And this is our last 'true' summer vacation—the last one where we don't *have* to work. Our last taste of true freedom!"

Needless to say, there's a reason why Curtis and Victor are my best friends.

"We had *plans*," Curtis went on. "We were going spelunking with my sister and her boyfriend. We were going to go scuba diving." Sure enough, we'd all gotten our dive permits earlier that year.

"And what about bike rides," I said, "and swimming at the pool and hiking in the woods?"

"Who knows?" Victor said. "We might have even hung out at the mall."

"The point is," Curtis said, "this summer was going to be the sweet life, and now it's not."

"But what can we do?" I said. "I mean, they're our *dads*."

Curtis thought for a second. Then, very quietly, he said, "We could lie. Say that we've taken summer jobs when we really haven't."

The walls of the bomb shelter were thick enough to muffle the screams of neighbors dying of radiation poisoning, but Curtis had whispered anyway. I knew why. What he was suggesting—lying to our parents—was A Very Big Deal.

Victor and I didn't say anything. The soft-serve ice-cream machine hummed. The watercooler gurgled.

Finally, I said, "That won't work. My dad's going to want to see the money I earn."

"Besides," Victor said, "I don't want to lie to my parents. About little things, sure. But this is a big thing."

"Yeah," Curtis said reluctantly.

We stared at the walls, at our framed posters for *Indiana Jones* and *Pirates of the Caribbean*—movies about adventures that we definitely wouldn't be having this summer. Remember when I said Curtis was like a clown fish, luring people into things they later regretted? The suggestion that we should lie to our parents—that was the poisonous sea anemone he was trying to lure me and Victor into. I knew it, and Victor knew it. So part of me was relieved that Victor and I had so quickly put the kibosh on Curtis's idea. That said, I couldn't stop thinking about how unfair it was that my dad was making me get a summer job. So another part of me wanted Curtis to keep talking.

And Curtis did. "Wait a minute," he said. "Our dads just said summer jobs, right? They didn't say *what* summer jobs."

"Yeah," Victor said. "So?"

"So what if we found some way to make all the money we *would have made* at our summer jobs? Like a onetime job with a big payoff? After all, it's about the money, not the actual work, right?"

"No," I said. "For my dad, I think it totally *is* about the actual work. And the people I supposedly meet along the way."

"Mine too," Victor said. "My dad says work builds character."

"Says them," Curtis said. "But if that's what our dads-slash-slavemasters are saying, then that's just stupid. It's already not fair we're being forced to make money we don't need. But it's *really* not fair if the only way we can make that money is through some dreary minimum-wage job. What about the creativity and smarts that we'd need to pull it off another way? Wouldn't that build character too? Shouldn't we get credit for *that*?"

"He has a point," I said to Victor. "How much money are we talking, anyway?"

"Well, figure six-fifty an hour for forty hours a week." Victor calculated. "That's two hundred and sixty dollars. And there are—what? Ten weeks from now until

Labor Day? But figure it takes at least a week to find a job. So two hundred and sixty dollars times nine weeks? That's about twenty-three hundred dollars we'd need to cover the whole summer."

"Times the three of us," I said. "So about seven thousand dollars."

"That's *it*?" Curtis said. "All we need is seven thousand dollars and we can take the whole summer off?"

"What do you have in mind?" I said. "Robbing a bank?"

"We don't need to rob a bank. We can get seven thousand dollars *easy*. First, how much money do we have right now?"

"Have?" I said.

"You know," Curtis said. "In savings."

"I have, like, six dollars in my wallet," I said. "Why would I have savings? That's the whole point of an allowance."

"I have some savings bonds," Victor said. "But my parents would never let me cash them in. Other than that, I have about four dollars and fifty cents." He looked at Curtis. "What about you?"

"I have forty-five left over from my birthday." He thought for a second. "Okay, so we'll have to earn the whole thing. But that's no problem. I mean, it might take a week or two, but still. How hard can it be?"

"You're forgetting something," Victor said. "Even if we do somehow make seven thousand dollars, our dads would still expect us to leave every day to go to our summer jobs."

"Piece-o-cake," Curtis said. "We just tell our dads that we *did* get jobs. And then we make up fake schedules and just be sure to come here at the right times so it looks like we're really working at our 'jobs.' My parents and sister work all day, so we don't have to worry about them seeing us come here."

"You mean we lie," Victor said.

"Yeah," he admitted, "but *little* lies. Remember, we *will* have a summer job. Of sorts. And we *will* make the money we would have made. And it's totally not fair they're making us do this in the first place!"

"So if my dad asks, I tell him I have a job working at KFC?" Victor said.

"Why not?" Curtis said. "We can pick you up a KFC

T-shirt somewhere, and you just have to come home every now and then with a bucket of chicken and maybe a Band-Aid from where you burned your hand on the deep fryer."

"I don't know if it'd be quite that easy," I said. After all, our dads were *surveyors*; wasn't the whole point that they *observe* things? My dad even sometimes joked about his "surveyor's sense," like Spider-Man's "spider sense"—a feeling he supposedly got whenever something was a little off.

"Sure it would!" Curtis said to me.

"What would your summer 'job' be?" Victor asked Curtis.

"Hmmm, I should do something outside," he said thoughtfully. "And something physical—my dad will think I'm building more character that way."

"How about horse wrangling?" I said.

"No," Curtis said. "I think maybe I'll mow the lawns at the country club." He looked at me. "Dave? What about you?"

"Well . . ." I considered my options. "I took lifesaving in school this year. And you only have to be fifteen to be a lifeguard."

"Presto!" Curtis announced, waving at me like a faith healer. "You're a lifeguard!"

"Okay, okay," Victor said. "We get fake jobs. Like you said, that's the easy part. How do we make the seven thousand dollars?"

"No, *that's* the easy part," Curtis said. "Trust me! This is *us* we're talking about, remember? But we may not even need the money."

"Huh?" Victor said, confused.

"You know our dads. Maybe they were just shootin' the breeze. Maybe they got all excited about us working, but by tomorrow they'll forget all about it."

Curtis had a point. Six months earlier, my dad had bought an expensive health club membership, went twice, and then suddenly experienced selective amnesia, in which all traces of the health club membership were suddenly and completely forgotten.

But two days later, over a dinner of hot-dog chili, my dad's eyes bored into me. "So," he said, "how goes the search for a summer job?"

In other words, he wasn't going to forget. Why would he? Unlike the episode with the health club membership, this time I was the one doing all the work.

"Uh," I said. "Not so good."

My dad sighed. "Dave, Dave, Dave."

This was too much. It was only the third day of summer vacation!

I thought about what Curtis, Victor, and I had talked about. Did I dare lie to my dad—even if it was just a little lie?

"I am thinking about applying to be a lifeguard down at the Fircrest Pool," I said. This was the local community pool, and what I'd said wasn't exactly a lie: When I did eventually end up getting a summer job, that was where I hoped it would be.

"Don't think," he said, shaking extra-mild hot sauce into his chili. "*Do it!*"

"My dad didn't forget," I said the next day, back in the bomb shelter.

"Mine either," Curtis said.

"Mine either," Victor said. "So does that mean the earn-seven-thousand-dollars-so-we-don't-have-to-get-summer-jobs project is a go?"

"Magic Eight Ball says 'Yes'!" Curtis said. He turned

the crank on our gum-ball machine, which we'd rigged so it didn't need money. "And mark my words: We'll have that seven thousand dollars in no time. But we need a name."

"A name?" I said.

"For this summer project of ours!" Curtis said. "We can't go around calling it the earn-seven-thousand-dollars-so-we-don't-have-to-get-summer-jobs project."

"I thought you said it was just a onetime thing," I said. "Why do we need a name for that?"

"How about Project Sweet Life?" Curtis said, ignoring my perfectly reasonable observation. "Because the sweet life is what the rest of our summer is gonna be once we get that money!"

Victor twitched. "How?"

"How what?" Curtis said, confidently gnawing on the gum ball and settling back into the oversize couch.

"How are we going to make seven thousand dollars?" Victor said. "You still haven't told us that. And I hope it goes without saying that whatever it is, it's got to be *legal*."

"It *does* go without saying," Curtis said. "Trust me, I have the perfect, and perfectly *legal*, idea for making the money we need."

"So?" Victor said. "What *is* it?"

"I can't tell you just yet. I need a little more time to work out the kinks." He started to blow a big bubble with the gum.

"When will you tell us?" Victor asked.

"I'll tell you all about it this weekend," Curtis said just as the green bubble popped in his face.

Friday night over a dinner of canned-tuna tacos, my dad asked me how it had gone with the lifeguard interview.

Suddenly the tuna smelled so bad, I thought I was going to throw up.

So this was it. Did I dare lie outright to my dad—fully and completely?

I thought about Project Sweet Life and what Curtis had said about having the "perfect" idea. I knew he'd been shading the truth again. But it was only seven thousand dollars. Curtis was right: How hard could getting that be?

I ignored the smell of the tacos and looked straight at my dad. "I got the job," I said. "I start tomorrow."

"Ha!" my dad said. "Thatta boy!" This is what he says to me on those incredibly rare occasions when he is actually proud of me.

There it was; I had officially lied to my dad. Now that I'd said out loud that I had a job, he was going to expect to see the money I was supposedly earning from it.

In other words, whether I liked it or not, I was now fully committed to Project Sweet Life.

WEEK 2:

The Junk-Free
No-Garage Garage Sale

The next day, Saturday, I told my parents I had to work. Lying didn't get any easier the second time around. But they didn't question me, especially since I left with a towel and a pair of swim trunks.

Instead of going to my "job" at the pool, I met Victor and Curtis and we went for a bike ride. Technically, Curtis, Victor, and I live just outside the city limits of Tacoma, Washington, in a suburb called Fircrest, where the pool is. It's so the burbs: yard gnomes and plastic birdbaths and cul-de-sacs everywhere you turn.

But we live in the older burbs—built in the sixties

and seventies. Since our families' houses were built, newer ones have sprung up beyond them. The houses are bigger, along with the SUVs, and the yards are smaller, landscaped with gravel and small patches of bright emerald-green lawn. The streets are eerily deserted, and everything seems to be hidden behind fences and gates. No matter where you go, it feels like you're in someone's back alley. In other words, these newer suburbs are somehow even more lifeless than the old ones.

But at least the streets have bike lanes, and they're always deserted, so that's where we went on our ride. The Fircrest Pool wasn't too far away, so if my parents drove by and saw me, I could say I was on my lunch break.

The time had come for Curtis to tell us how to earn the seven thousand dollars for Project Sweet Life. I was pretty sure he hadn't come up with an idea, because if he had he wouldn't have wasted any time telling us. But I didn't want to ruin the day by pointing that out.

To my relief, Victor was the one who finally brought it up.

We were passing through the parking lot of one of those cinder-block strip malls when Victor said to Curtis, "So? It's the weekend. What's this great idea you have for making seven thousand dollars?"

Curtis skidded to a halt. *"Estate sale!"*

"Huh?" I said, rolling to a stop. I turned back to look at him.

Curtis pointed to a storefront. "Look! They're holding an estate sale."

Sure enough, there was a sign in the window announcing an estate sale in big red letters.

"Let's check it out," Curtis said.

I knew Curtis was totally avoiding Victor's question. But I also knew we'd check out that estate sale. We always did. It's one way we'd ended up with all that cool stuff in our bomb shelter.

We locked up our bikes and went inside.

"This looks like a pretty big sale," I said.

"I just overheard someone talking," Curtis said. "It's the estate of some local bigwig. Government guy."

If it really was the estate of some rich guy, most of the expensive stuff must have already been sold. What we saw was lots of junk: dishes and a blender and books and a coffeemaker and magazines spread out over long cafeteria tables in no particular order. Bargain hunters flitted between the tables. In an estate sale, the owner is dead, and I couldn't help but be reminded of that scene in *A Christmas Carol* where the servants are laughing about taking the curtains right from the bed where Scrooge's corpse lay.

"Curtis," Victor said patiently. "You didn't answer my question. What's your idea for how we're going to make seven thousand dollars?"

Curtis joined the browsers at the nearest table. "Hey, look at this!" he said, pointing to a twelve-inch-tall ceramic statue of Mr. Moneybags, the cartoon millionaire character from the Monopoly board game. It had the familiar top hat and handlebar mustache, and the arms were outstretched with a cane in one hand.

Curtis checked the price tag. "It's only two dollars!" he said. "I'm so buying it. It's a perfect mascot for Project Sweet Life."

"Great," Victor said patiently. "Now what's your idea?"

But Curtis was already on to another table. "And look at *this*," Curtis said. He held up a book called *Trains and Totem Poles: A History of Tacoma, Washington*. It had a photograph of Old City Hall, a local landmark, on the cover.

Victor looked over at me and rolled his eyes. I nodded. Curtis was usually good at shading the truth, but not always.

"Curtis," Victor said. "Stop."

"What?" He did stop, on the opposite side of the table. But that didn't mean he looked at us.

"You don't have any idea how we're going to make seven thousand dollars, do you?" Victor said.

"I do *so*!" Curtis said indignantly. But he still wasn't looking us in the eye.

"So?" Victor said. "*How?*"

Curtis stared down at the flatware. Then he looked up at us with a big grin. "We hold a garage sale," he said smugly.

A garage sale? That was Curtis's idea to make seven thousand dollars?

Victor was even less impressed than I was. "How are we going to make seven thousand dollars at a *garage sale*? Besides, you obviously just thought of it this very minute."

"So?" Curtis said.

"So earlier you said you *already* had the perfect idea,

that you just needed to work out the kinks."

"What difference does it make? I came up with a great idea, didn't I?"

"*Did* you?" I said. "How are we going to make the money we need at a garage sale? I've never heard of anyone making anywhere near that much."

"Ah, but this won't be like any other garage sale!" Curtis said excitedly. "Look around you! Most garage and estate sales, sell *everything*—and most of it turns out to be complete junk." He nodded to the nearest table. "I mean, wire hangers? Ice-cube trays? Come *on*. This is *garbage*. But we *won't* be selling garbage!"

"What will we be selling?" Victor said evenly.

"Good stuff!" Curtis said. "All the great stuff we have in the bomb shelter. With stuff like that, making seven thousand dollars will be a piece-o-cake."

It was true that we'd collected some pretty great stuff over the years. But it hadn't come easy. Did he want us to just give it all up? The flat-screen television and game system? The mini-refrigerator? The movie-style popcorn popper? The *couch*?

"But that's . . ." Victor said. "You know. Our stuff." He sounded as reluctant as I felt.

"But it'd be for one last summer of freedom!" Curtis said. "Remember? How much is that freedom worth to you? And don't forget, it's not like we don't get anything out of it. We sell our stuff, then we'll have seven thousand dollars we can use to buy *new* stuff."

"But what if it's not enough?" I asked. We had great stuff in the bomb shelter, true, but I didn't see how all of it put together could be worth seven grand.

An image of the plasma lamp back in my bedroom flashed through my mind. We might make it to seven thousand dollars, I realized, if the three of us also sold our personal possessions. It was kind of incredible what a kid could accumulate over the years even without a job, what with birthdays and Christmases and graduations. But would I really have to give up my plasma lamp? At night in my bedroom, long after I'd turned out the other lights, I loved to watch the purple bolts snake around the interior of the glass globe.

"It *will* be enough," Curtis said, and I couldn't help but wonder if some favorite personal belonging had flashed through *his* mind.

"But even if we did have this great garage sale, where would we hold it?" Victor said, and I was glad he was changing the subject. "We can't have it at any of our houses, or our parents will know where we got the money, and then it won't count toward our summer jobs."

On this point, even Curtis was stumped.

But that's when I had an idea. "I think I know who can help us," I said.

Uncle Brad is my dad's brother, but they really couldn't be more different. If everything is black-and-white for my dad, Uncle Brad definitely tends toward the colorful. For example, when asked to bring food to a party, most people might show up with salsa and a bag of corn chips; Uncle Brad brings tropical chicken on sugarcane skewers with a peanut-plantain dipping sauce. For Christmas gifts, most people give gift cards to Barnes & Noble or Target; Uncle Brad gives signed first editions of *Charlie and the Chocolate Factory* and, well, purple plasma lamps.

Uncle Brad lives with his friend Uncle Danny in a house they've fixed up in the North End, the old part of town. Just like Uncle Brad is the opposite of my dad, the North End is the opposite of where we live. It's the kind of neighborhood where most of the houses have at least one stained-glass window and the roots of the old trees have gotten so thick, they've started to tear up the sidewalks. My parents' part of town doesn't even *have* sidewalks.

The next afternoon, Sunday, Curtis, Victor, and I rode our bikes over to visit my uncles.

"Dave!" Uncle Brad said at the front door. "What brings you and your friends here?" Uncle Brad looks like a more relaxed version of my dad, with longer hair and a looser posture. Uncle Danny, who joined us from the kitchen, is tall and slender with silver hair.

"We need to ask a favor," I said.

"Sure," Uncle Brad said. "Come on in."

The inside of their house reminded me of our bomb shelter—sort of a clubhouse for adults, with Persian rugs and crown molding and lots of candles and hanging houseplants. The air smelled like cinnamon and Elmer's glue, probably from one of my uncles' craft projects.

I didn't beat around the bush. "We want to hold a garage sale next weekend, and we were wondering if we could use your garage."

"Actually, no," Uncle Brad said.

"Oh," I said. This was embarrassing.

Uncle Brad smiled. "We rent our garage to one of our neighbors, and he's kind of particular about it. But you might be able to use our front porch."

"Really?"

"Assuming you tell us why. Why not one of your own garages?"

"We figured we'd make more money here," Curtis said. "Since this is a richer part of town."

"I see," Uncle Brad said. "Trying to keep it from your parents, huh?"

Unfortunately for us, my uncles are not stupid.

I looked at Curtis and Victor. They both shrugged, so I explained to my uncles all about Project Sweet Life.

Uncle Brad and Uncle Danny eyed each other, smiling. Then Uncle Danny snickered, and Uncle Brad joined in. Soon they'd completely busted up.

I let them laugh for a moment. Then I said, "I know you guys think this is very funny. And why wouldn't you? We're just a bunch of teenagers, right? Why should our problems count for anything?" I turned to Curtis and Victor. "Come on. I guess I was wrong about my uncles. Let's get out of here."

We started for the door. The floor creaked. Behind us, I could sense Uncle Brad and Uncle Danny looking at each other.

"Wait," Uncle Brad said.

We waited.

"You are absolutely right," he went on. "I can't believe we laughed at you. I used to hate it when adults did that to me. We are so sorry."

"And of course you can use our porch," Uncle Danny said. "When will you need it?"

"Next Saturday from ten to five," I said without missing a beat. "If it's okay, we also need you to help us drive everything over here so we can store it in your basement until then. And we'll stop by Friday night to put signs up around the neighborhood."

Uncle Danny was the first to smile again. "We just totally got played, didn't we?"

"Totally," I admitted.

Tuesday was the Fourth of July. Since the whole point of Project Sweet Life was for us to have one last summer of freedom, we were determined not to miss the most important holiday of the season.

We began the day traveling between our three houses, from the chaotic madhouse that is a holiday at Victor's, to the plastic perfection of Curtis's family, to the little piece of Americana that is my own parents. Everywhere we went, the adults wanted to know the same thing:

"How do you like working at KFC?" Curtis's dad asked Victor.

"How do you like working at the country club?" my dad asked Curtis.

"How do you like being a lifeguard?" Victor's dad asked me.

I think even Curtis was taken aback by the verbal onslaught. Since when did their teenage sons' summer jobs become such fascinating barbecue conversation? No amount of apple pie and homemade ice cream was worth this, so the three of us took off again on our bikes.

By early evening, we'd ridden back to the North End and down to the waterfront, where the city puts on a big fireworks show over the bay. We climbed a big oak tree at the edge of a greenbelt and had a perfect view of all the boats in the water below us and the indigo sky above. The air smelled of cut grass and barbecue smoke. Finally, we could relax.

Once the fireworks began, we watched wordlessly. When they were over, no one moved. We just kept watching the sky as the gray smoke slowly faded. In the distance, cars were already honking impatiently as they inched their way through the gridlock that now encased the entire waterfront. Even that was soothing in a way, because it seemed to be coming from a world apart.

"It's not enough," I said quietly.

"What isn't?" Victor said.

I squirmed upright on my branch. "The stuff in the bomb shelter. Even if we do sell it all, we won't make seven thousand dollars." I hated to inject reality back into the night, but someone had to say it.

"Yes, we *will*," Curtis said. "We just have to have faith."

"What are you saying?" Victor said to me.

"I'm saying we need to sell our personal stuff too," I said. "Everything." *Even*, I thought, *my purple plasma lamp*.

My words hung in the air like the golden trail of a skyrocket right before the final explosion. They were just that obvious, and the conclusion was just that inevitable.

"Everything?" Curtis asked, and I suddenly knew

exactly what he was picturing in his head: his *Star Wars* Bounty Hunter Action Figure set, still in its original box and signed by the actor who had played Boba Fett.

"Everything," I said.

"*Everything?*" Victor said. I was certain he was thinking of his Meade Deep Space Telescope.

"Well," I said, losing my nerve. "Maybe not *everything*." Maybe if he got to keep his telescope, I'd get to keep my purple plasma lamp.

"No," Curtis said. "Are we committed to Project Sweet Life or not? Do we want freedom or not? Because a lot of people *say* they want freedom, but they don't really mean it. They'd rather have things."

We all thought about this for a moment.

Then I said, "Curtis is right."

Victor didn't answer.

"Victor?" I asked him.

"Okay, okay, I'm in," he mumbled. "But holy Parsimonious, patron saint of tightwads, this garage sale better work."

So began our preparation for the Project Sweet Life Junk-Free No-Garage Garage Sale.

We. Were. Ruthless.

After all, Curtis was right: How did you put a price on freedom?

We started with everything in the bomb shelter: the television, the game system, the popcorn popper, the Sno-Kone maker, the soft-serve and gum-ball machines, the posters on the walls, the watercooler, the refrigerator, and the couch. We also stripped the bomb shelter itself of anything we thought might have nostalgic appeal: the dilapidated power generator, an ancient air filter, some old bottles and canned food with the labels more or less intact, a cistern, metal shelves, and the kitschy 1960s bomb shelter signs. We didn't tell Curtis's parents about this, but they hadn't seen the inside of the shelter in about ten years, so we knew they didn't care. When we were done we no longer had a hideout; we had a concrete pillbox.

After that, we turned our attention to our individual bedrooms and our own personal worldly possessions. I knew that in their bedrooms, Curtis and Victor were packing up telescopes and *Star Wars* Bounty Hunter Action Figure boxed sets.

In my own bedroom, I picked up my four-foot ana-tomically correct plastic ant. I put it in the "to sell" box.

I lovingly caressed the fog machine that had enabled me to make some of the best haunted houses this side of Disney World. Then I boxed it up.

Finally, I came to my purple plasma lamp. I boxed that up, too.

By the time I was done packing my possessions, my shelves and closet were almost completely bare. Knowing this would have made our parents suspicious, we'd gone to Goodwill and collected stuff from the "free" bins— mostly coverless paperbacks and broken knickknacks. So now I replaced my good stuff with the free stuff, knowing my clueless parents would never suspect a thing.

It wasn't easy sneaking everything out of my house without my parents knowing, especially since, unlike Curtis's mom, my mom is home all day. It was even worse for Victor, who had the dreaded nosy little siblings. But we managed, and by Friday night, we had everything stored over in the basement at Uncle Brad and Uncle Danny's. Then we posted flyers everywhere within a ten-block radius of their house.

Curtis's garage sale idea wasn't a bad one, even if he had pulled it out of thin air. We had Good Stuff. If I'd come to our garage sale, I would have wanted to buy absolutely everything there. But that made sense, since it was *my* stuff and that of my friends. The question was, would anyone else agree?

Saturday morning dawned bright and beautiful, like a sunrise in one of those calendars full of cheesy inspirational phrases. I told my parents I was off to work.

"Thatta boy," my dad said.

My mom smiled. "Watch out for sharks."

It still felt weird to lie to them so brazenly, and I did feel bad about it. But I reminded myself that this was all my dad's fault to begin with, that he was basically *forcing* me to lie with his totally unfair insistence that I get a summer job. Even so, what would happen if they happened to drive by Uncle Brad and Uncle Danny's place and saw me there? Or what if someone from Curtis's or Victor's family drove by? How would we ever explain it? That said, we only needed to get through this one day, then we could spend the rest of the summer doing whatever we wanted. It's not like we were going to run into any of our family members at most of our usual haunts.

It was still early by the time Curtis, Victor, and I arrived at Uncle Brad and Uncle Danny's. We had time to set up big wooden sandwich boards on the surrounding streets, directing people to our sale.

By now, anyone even remotely interested in garage sales had to know about ours. But just to make sure, I took all of our leftover cardboard boxes and made a huge, eye-catching tower out of them in front of Uncle Brad and Uncle Danny's garage.

"Wait!" Curtis said. He grabbed the statue of Mr. Moneybags that he'd bought the weekend before.

"Shouldn't we sell that too?" Victor asked.

"Bite your tongue depressor!" Curtis said. "We can't sell our mascot. Besides, it cost two whole bucks."

He climbed up on a chair to place it on top of the tower of cardboard like a Christmas star. "There," he said.

Well before we officially opened at ten, the bargain vultures were already circling. Somehow they had sensed that this garage sale was different. We were ready for them, with a wide selection of carefully chosen, genuinely valuable stuff, reasonably priced with just enough leeway to allow for some haggling.

At ten on the dot, the bartering began. It felt weird watching our most prized possessions being lugged away from the porch. I got the impression that the lumpy housewife who bought my copy of Pauline Baynes's original 1972 map of Narnia just wanted it for the frame. And what the heck was a nine-year-old girl going to do with a six-channel Raptor G-2 remote-controlled helicopter? But the blow of losing all that stuff was definitely softened by the wad of cash that kept growing in our strongbox.

Unlike most garage sales, which start strong and peter out as the day wears on and the worthwhile merchandise gets carted away, our crowd actually began to grow, especially among the under-twenty set. Word had apparently gotten out that we'd lost our marbles. Before we knew it, the front porch was thronged, and Curtis, Victor, and I were doing a land-office business.

Mr. Moneybags was definitely watching over us from the top of that cardboard tower. By the afternoon, Curtis, Victor, and I all had little dollar signs in place of our eyes.

"Count it!" Curtis said once almost everything had been sold (even the antique generator, and for a surprisingly generous amount).

"I'm counting," Victor said.

Curtis and I watched silently until he finally announced, "Five thousand, eight hundred."

"Dollars?" Curtis asked.

"No, Italian lira!" Victor said. "Yes, dollars—what'd you think I meant?"

I could hardly believe my ears. We didn't have the full seven thousand dollars, but we had most of it! We could earn the rest of what we needed washing windows over a long weekend.

"We did it," I said, finding my tongue at last. "Curtis, you were right! It was so easy! And we now have almost six thousand dollars!"

"Didn't I tell you?" Curtis said. "Piece-o-cake!"

At that moment, Uncle Brad's garage began to squeak from the inside, like someone had activated the remote control on the door. Sure enough, the garage door rumbled open to reveal the back of a sleek red Ferrari. Uncle Brad and Uncle Danny's neighbor, a red-faced man with pasty white legs, sauntered toward his car, keys jingling in his hand.

"What the—?" He'd noticed our tower of cardboard boxes right in front of his car.

"Sorry," said Curtis from the front porch. "We'll

get that out of your way."

Victor was the first one to reach the tower. He went to push it to one side. But I hadn't built it as solidly as I'd thought, and it was only cardboard boxes to begin with.

It teetered.

"Whoa!" Victor said, even as he tried valiantly to keep it from toppling over. But it was too late. It started to fall backward toward the open garage.

I remembered the ceramic statue of Mr. Moneybags that Curtis had placed at the top.

A ceramic statue that was heading right for the back of that red Ferrari.

I held my breath. Time seemed to stop.

Unfortunately, it didn't stay stopped.

The Mr. Moneybags statue crashed down against the Ferrari, denting the trunk and cracking the back window.

Six thousand dollars. Since it was a luxury car (and since the owner was preoccupied with his insurance rates), that's what we learned it would cost us to repair. But that pretty much figured, didn't it?

Uncle Brad offered to pay for the damage, but the

most we would take from him was the two-hundred-dollar difference between what we'd earned and what we owed—and only as a loan. After all, he and Uncle Danny had been doing us a favor by letting us use their porch—and they'd only done it because we'd insisted that we be treated as adults. Curtis, Victor, and I had all been equally involved in the mishap with the statue: I'd built the cardboard tower, Curtis had put the statue on top, and Victor had knocked it over. So it was only fair that we all paid for the damage.

But none of that made it any easier to accept. Project Sweet Life, our simple, brilliant plan to get out of working over the summer, had only been in operation for a week. And we were already two hundred dollars in the hole.

WEEK 3:

Robberies in Plain Sight

The next day, Tuesday, I told my parents I'd be at work and headed over to the bomb shelter for a post-garage-sale conference. The shelter itself had been stripped completely bare. The only things left were that statue of Mr. Moneybags, which we had decided to keep as our mascot despite the bad luck it had already brought us, and *Trains and Totem Poles*, the book on the history of Tacoma that Curtis had also bought at the estate sale. I'd known the bomb shelter was made of concrete, but I'd never realized that it was *just* concrete, not until we'd sold all our stuff. It had never smelled dusty and dirty before either, but it did now.

Victor was sulking.

"Oh, come *on*," Curtis said. "So we didn't make seven thousand dollars the first time out. We *almost* did! It just goes to show that Project Sweet Life is going to be even easier than we thought."

"I'm not mad because we didn't make seven thousand dollars the first time out," Victor said. "I'm mad because we didn't make seven thousand dollars *and* I no longer have all my favorite stuff that you made me sell."

This made me feel guilty. I was the one, not Curtis, who had first suggested that we sell all of our personal belongings.

"Well," Curtis said, "ignore all that."

"How can we ignore it?" Victor said. "Our *couch* is gone. We don't even have a place to *sit*."

"Just listen, okay?" Curtis said. "I have a new plan. And this one is guaranteed to succeed!"

"That's what you said about the *last* plan," Victor mumbled.

Curtis ignored him. "Where do most people go when

44

they want a lot of money? To the bank."

"Wait," I said. "You want to rob a bank? I was kidding about that."

"I don't want to *rob* a bank," Curtis said. "I want to keep a bank from *being* robbed."

Curtis's words echoed inside the empty bomb shelter. I sat up, intrigued, even though the hard floor hurt the bones in my rear end.

"Tell me more," I said.

"I did a little research on Capitol American Bank, which has a branch just down the street," Curtis said. "It turns out they pay a hundred-thousand-dollar reward for information that leads to the capture and arrest of any bank robber."

"What are you saying? That one of us robs the bank so the other two can turn him in?" I slumped back down.

"Not us," Curtis said. "An actual bank robber! We catch him or provide information that leads to his arrest, and we make ourselves a fast hundred thousand dollars."

"Curtis," Victor said. "You're not making sense. What makes you think anyone's going to rob that bank?"

"Because that particular branch has already been robbed twice in the last six months!"

Victor and I looked at each other.

"How?" I said. "No one robs banks anymore. They have Plexiglas and hidden cameras. And if the bank has been robbed twice in six months, wouldn't they have a security guard?"

"All true," Curtis said. "That's why it's not the bank itself that's being robbed. It's people who come to pick up money. The first time, it was this man who withdrew cash for some business deal. The thief followed him home and robbed him there. The second time it was a woman who'd taken some diamonds from her safe-deposit box. The thief followed her home too. Anyway, that's why I think this was an *inside job*."

"An inside job?" I said. "What are you talking about?"

"Think about it. Both robberies were perfectly timed. Whoever robbed that man and woman knew exactly what they'd taken from the bank. In other words, it had to be someone inside the bank working with someone on the outside!"

What Curtis said did make sense. I stared at the statue of Mr. Moneybags on the floor next to me. For the record, Mr. Moneybags hadn't even been chipped in the fall against that Ferrari.

"How do you know all this?" I asked Curtis.

"My mom knows someone who knows someone who works at the bank," Curtis said.

It wasn't exactly the most impressive source.

"Do those even count as bank 'robberies' as far as the reward is concerned?" Victor said. "They sound more like people who just happened to get ripped off."

"My mom says the bank is treating them like bank robberies because they took place so soon after their customers went to the bank," Curtis said. "They want to catch the thief more than anyone. They don't want people to pull their money out of that branch."

"Even if this is all true," I said, "how would *we* catch the bank robber?"

"We do a stakeout," Curtis said. "Somewhere in front of the bank."

"Yeah, we could take a video of the robbery," Victor said. "Oh, wait, no, we can't! I don't have a camcorder anymore—I sold it at our pointless garage sale!"

"I don't know *exactly* how we'll catch the robber," Curtis said. "Just that we *will*."

47

"*Eventually*, you mean?" Victor said. "If that bank is only robbed once every three months, doesn't that mean we might have to watch it all summer long? I thought the whole point of Project Sweet Life was that we end up with a sweet life. How is this better than an actual summer job?"

"It pays a hundred thousand dollars, for one thing," Curtis said. "Look, can we just go check it out?"

We rode our bikes over to Capitol American Bank. It happened to be the branch where I had my own bank account (currently nearly empty, alas). It was located in the newer suburbs, on a busy street—the kind with five fat, SUV-friendly lanes, but no sidewalks. The bank itself was small with big glass windows along the street. There was a small parking lot to one side.

We locked up our bikes and went inside. The front part of the bank had a small waiting area and some desks separated by low-rise cubicle walls; the tellers worked in the back behind a row of Plexiglas windows. The vault with the safe-deposit boxes was behind a railing to the left of the teller windows. We saw seven employees— three managers, three tellers, and a flabby security guard.

But there is only so long that three teenagers can linger in a bank without people getting suspicious, so we left. Plus, this was my parents' branch, and I didn't want to accidentally run into them.

Outside, Curtis nodded at the coffee shop across the street. "Let's go sit," he said.

The coffee shop was one of those old-fashioned diners with a counter and stools and metal napkin dispensers, where every surface feels vaguely sticky. I found myself wondering who still ate in greasy spoons like this. We took a booth by the window. I could tell that Curtis had something to say, but before he could speak, a waitress handed us menus.

"Get you boys somethin' to drink?" she said. Her skin was deeply tanned, and her teeth were unnaturally white. If you squinted, she might not have looked too old. But we weren't squinting.

"Just water," Curtis said, declining the menu.

"Me too," Victor said, scrutinizing the grease on the vinyl seat.

The fact was, money was tight for the three of us. We'd given all the money from the garage sale to the guy with the Ferrari. And even though we'd started out the summer with a little over fifty-five dollars between us, Curtis had bought that book and statue at the estate sale, and Victor had had to drop ten bucks on a KFC T-shirt, leaving us with a grand total of $41.50—money that had to last until we made the seven thousand dollars we needed for Project Sweet Life.

Still, I said to the waitress, "I'll have a small Coke." If we were going to sit in this coffee shop, it seemed like we should order *something*.

The waitress just smiled gamely.

When she was gone, Curtis said, "It's Gladys Kravitz! I bet she's the bank robber!"

"Who?" I said, confused.

"That bank manager who looks like the nosy neighbor on *Bewitched*?"

We all looked back over at the bank. From the window of the coffee shop, we had a good view inside.

I'd never really watched *Bewitched*, but I could tell by the name that Gladys Kravitz was frumpy, and one of the bank managers fit the bill. You could almost see the curlers in her hair.

"What makes you think it's her?" I asked.

"Something about her eyes," he said. "Shifty."

I laughed, but Victor said, "I think we need a little more to go on than that."

"This is *amazing*," Curtis said, still staring over at the bank. "You can see everything from here."

He wasn't kidding. Thanks to the glass windows of the bank, this coffee shop was the perfect spot to observe what was going on across the street. It was like looking into an ant farm, except with lazier workers.

"That's it!" Curtis said.

"What's it?" I said.

"This coffee shop is where we can do our stakeout! We can sit right at this table until we know for sure that Gladys Kravitz is the bank robber. We could even take shifts."

"Yeah, and we could call each other on our walkie-talkies," Victor said bitterly. "Except—oh wait! We sold those at our pointless garage sale."

"How would that work?" I said to Curtis. "Even if Gladys Kravitz *is* the bank robber, Victor was right when he said it might be weeks or months before she strikes again."

But Curtis's eyes were still locked on the bank. "Guys?" he said. "There's something going on over there."

Victor and I both turned to look, but I didn't see anything strange.

"What?" Victor said.

"That woman!" Curtis said. "Not Gladys Kravitz. The one with the orange pants and the big butt."

I zeroed in on the woman with the orange pants (she really did have an enormous rear end). She stood in a tiny cubicle on the far right side of the bank, behind the loan officers' desks. It was a little office area with a copy machine and fax. Like all the work spaces, it had cubicle walls, but they were higher than the others. The only way we were able to see her was because we were on the outside looking in through the window.

Even so, I didn't see what the big deal was. She was talking on her cell phone.

"What about her?" I asked.

"It looks like she's *whispering*," Curtis said.

Needless to say, Curtis has a tendency to jump to conclusions. Still, it did look like the woman in the orange pants was whispering. It was something about how she was hunched over.

"And why is Happy Pants talking on a cell phone

anyway?" Curtis went on. "There's a phone on the desk right next to her."

This was also true.

"Maybe they don't allow personal calls on company phones," Victor said.

"It looks like she's *hiding*," Curtis said.

Curtis was right about this too. She was crouched down behind the office divider, but she kept glancing back toward the main office area.

"Maybe they don't allow personal calls on company time," Victor amended.

Suddenly Gladys Kravitz stood up from her desk and walked toward the copy machine.

Happy Pants spotted her coming and punched off her phone, sliding it into her purse. When Gladys Kravitz entered the copy area, Happy Pants fumbled for the stapler. You could almost hear the stilted small talk as she did her best to act casual.

I was wondering where this stapler was! she seemed to be saying. *I've been looking all over for it because, you know, I really need to staple something!*

She was *nervous*. But why?

Curtis looked at us as if to say, *Well?*

It seemed an impossible coincidence that we'd see something even vaguely suspicious after staking out the bank for ten minutes. I mean, what were the odds?

Still, we spent the rest of the afternoon watching the bank. We didn't see anything else out of the ordinary, but our attention had been piqued, so I knew we'd be back.

"Dave," my mom said that night as I passed by the kitchen where she was making a pot of her trademark pizza soup. "I'm really proud of you."

"Proud?" I said. "For what?"

"For getting that lifeguarding job." She dropped sliced pepperoni into the tomato sauce.

"Oh," I said. Suddenly it was all I could do to get out of that kitchen. I mean, my dad had been completely wrong to force me to get a job at age fifteen. But when someone compliments you for something you didn't do, for something that you have, in fact, totally lied about—well, you can't help feeling guilty.

"I know you didn't want a job," she said. "I know all the plans you and your friends had this summer. But you did it anyway, and you didn't even complain."

"Well," I said. "What can you do?"

I started to leave again, but my mom stopped me. "It really proves how mature you've become."

Okay, I thought, *enough already!* Was this really how she had thought of me? Not mature?

"Oh, as long as you're here," she said, starting to grate mozzarella cheese for us to sprinkle on top of the soup, "would you mind taking the garbage out?"

This reminded me that even though my parents had stopped my allowance, I was still expected to do all my chores. For free, apparently.

I grabbed the garbage from under the sink. Suddenly I didn't feel quite so guilty about lying anymore.

Curtis, Victor, and I met late the next morning at the coffee shop across from the bank.

"I'm sure what we saw yesterday was nothing," I said as we locked up our bikes. "We probably shouldn't get our hopes up."

"Says you," Curtis said. "It's a robbery. A robbery in plain sight."

We sat at the same table as before. The same waitress took our order.

"Just water," I said. Yesterday's Coke had pretty much broken the bank for me.

"Water," Victor said.

But Curtis announced to the waitress, "I'll have a Coke. *And* a side order of fries." In other words, he was so confident we'd catch this bank robber that he was willing to spend another four dollars of his—*our*—money.

The waitress just smiled, as if to say, *Whoa, big spender*.

Over in the bank, everything looked pretty much the same as the day before. Gladys Kravitz and Happy Pants were both working quietly at their desks.

It turns out that banks have a lunch-hour rush, so things were very busy for an hour or so. Then business slowed down, which was when the bank employees started to take *their* lunches, in shifts.

The coffee shop, however, *didn't* have a lunch-hour rush. That answered my question about who still ate in a greasy spoon like this: not many people. But all this thinking about food reminded me how hungry I was.

Curtis's French fries were long gone, and even burned split pea soup smells good when you've barely eaten since breakfast. But even Curtis's self-confidence had its limit, so we just sat there sipping our ice water. After a while, the waitress stopped asking us if we wanted anything else. To her credit, she never stopped refilling our waters.

"This is embarrassing," I said as the afternoon wore on and the waitress had filled our glasses for the hundredth time. "We can't sit at this table forever."

"They'll forgive us once we finger Happy Pants!" Curtis said, still staring at the bank. "We can come back here later and drop some serious cash."

"Curtis," Victor said quietly. "Dave is right. It's not just the embarrassment factor. We've been here for over four hours. This is *boring*."

"But what about what we saw yesterday?"

"We didn't see *anything* yesterday. We saw a woman using her cell phone."

Curtis clutched the tabletop like a desperate drunk being told he had to leave the bar. "Let's just stay till the bank closes at five. Can we at least do that?"

Victor and I looked at each other. We both knew that

if we didn't let Curtis get his way, we'd never hear the end of it.

"Okay," I said.

Curtis turned back to the window again, as if the sheer power of his scowl could force the occupants of the bank to do something incriminating.

As the minutes wore on, Curtis kept glaring at the bank, though Victor and I spent more time watching the clock on the wall of the coffee shop. The seats in our booth were padded, but they'd long since stopped feeling soft (though they were still just as sticky).

By five minutes to five, the diner was deserted except for Curtis, Victor, me, and a little old lady primly eating a BLT with a knife and fork.

I arched my back and stretched my arms.

"No," Curtis said firmly, without even looking at me. "Not yet."

"Curtis," Victor said. "Give it up."

"But what about the hundred-thousand-dollar *reward*? We have to catch those *robbers!*"

At the sound of Curtis's outburst, the old lady looked over at us. I grinned apologetically at her, and she returned to her BLT.

"Curtis?" I said patiently. "It's over."

"Wait," he said. "Wait! Something's happening!"

But Curtis had already cried wolf so many times that day that I didn't even turn.

"Please!" he implored. "Just *look*!"

So I looked. And Curtis was right: Something *was* happening inside the bank.

There was a woman who seemed to be asking about her safe-deposit box. All afternoon, people had been visiting their safe-deposit boxes, going in and out of the bank vault. But something about this woman was different. She didn't just look rich; she looked like she wanted people to *know* she was rich. She wore an all-white pantsuit and was as skinny as a department-store mannequin, and she posed like one too. With the exception of her actual face, anywhere she had bare skin—ears, neck, wrists, ankles— she wore shimmering gold jewelry.

When watching people through a window, you obviously don't know what they're saying to each other. But after a while, you start to think you do.

But it's not five o'clock yet! Golden Girl seemed to be saying to the bank teller.

Five o'clock is the time the bank closes, the bank teller seemed to reply. *That means all transactions need to be finished by then.*

I will be finished! Golden Girl said. *This will only take a second!*

I'm sorry, ma'am! the bank teller responded. *We stop access to the safe-deposit boxes at four forty-five.*

"Fascinating," Victor said sarcastically. "Curtis, what exactly does it say that *this* is the highlight of our afternoon?"

"Wait!" he said. "*Look!*"

He pointed over to the other end of the bank, to where Happy Pants had her desk.

She'd stopped what she was doing and was intently watching the interaction between Golden Girl and the bank teller.

"Curtis," I said, "if I worked there, I'd be watching that, too."

Suddenly Happy Pants twitched.

I didn't say anything, because I didn't want to encourage Curtis. But it looked like a nervous twitch.

Naturally Curtis saw it too. "There!" he said. "Did you see that? She's nervous about something!"

Happy Pants looked away from the interaction with Golden Girl, through the window of the bank to the street outside. What was she looking at? It wasn't us, like in that movie *Rear Window*, where the killer looks over and sees Jimmy Stewart spying on him through the window.

I looked back into the bank, at the vault where Golden Girl was still arguing with the teller. Knowing what I knew about rich people, I had a good idea what would happen. And sure enough, the clerk finally did relent, nodding and grudgingly letting Golden Girl in through the little swinging door that led back to the vault.

Happy Pants stood up from her desk and crossed toward the front doors.

"*Now* what is Happy Pants doing?" Curtis said.

I had to admit, this was interesting. Or did Curtis just have me jumping to conclusions now too?

As Golden Girl disappeared into the vault, Happy Pants slipped outside the bank to the little concrete plaza between the building and the parking lot.

Victor adjusted his glasses. "Where is she going?"

"We'll see in a minute!" Curtis said. "Now shhhhh!"

"What 'shhhhh'? We're across a busy street and inside

another building. How could she hear us?"

Right then, Happy Pants looked over, right at us, just like in *Rear Window*. We all flinched at exactly the same time.

"She's not looking at us," Curtis hurried to say. "There's a glare on these windows. She can't even see us."

I wasn't sure if this was true or not—after all, we'd been able to see *them* all afternoon. In any event, Happy Pants didn't keep looking at us. Instead, she hurried across the little plaza to the curb in front of the bank where a vendor was selling flowers out of a bucket.

They exchanged a few quick words, and she nodded to a particular bouquet. He handed her the flowers, and she palmed him some money.

"Get you boys anything more?" the waitress said suddenly.

We all jumped in surprise.

We'd been so caught up in the events across the street that we hadn't noticed her.

"What?" Curtis said. "No! Nothing, thanks!"

The waitress sighed loudly before disappearing again.

I wasn't sure what had finally gotten her so bent out of shape.

We turned back to the bank where Happy Pants was now hurrying inside with her flowers.

"That's it!" Curtis said. "That's the signal! Now the flower vendor is going to follow the woman in the white pantsuit so he can rob her of whatever she takes out of her safe-deposit box."

"But why bother with the flowers?" I said. "Why not just call him on her cell phone?"

"Because of all the security cameras in the bank," Curtis said. "If she used her cell phone, it might be obvious when they investigate that she was in on the crime. I bet they change their signal every time they rob someone new!"

"What do we do now?" I said. "Call the police?"

"We could use my cell phone," Victor said. "But oh, wait! I sold it at our pointless garage sale!"

"Would you *let it go*!" Curtis hissed at Victor. "We're about to capture a bunch of bank robbers. When we get that hundred-thousand-dollar reward, you'll be able to buy a hundred cell phones."

"But we need to call the police!" I said, lurching up from the table.

"Wait! Something else is happening," Curtis said.

I looked back at the bank. Golden Girl had slinked out of the building and was sashaying across the little plaza. Whatever she had taken from her safe-deposit box was small enough to fit inside her purse.

Meanwhile, there was a bustle of activity inside the bank. All of the tellers had left their Plexiglas cages and one of them was locking up the front doors. The loan officers had emerged from their cubicles too. It was five o'clock, but it didn't seem like anyone was leaving. It was more like they were lingering, waiting for something to happen.

It seemed like Gladys Kravitz was somehow the center of attention, even if she didn't know it exactly.

Then one of the tellers emerged from a door in the back of the bank carrying a white cake with candles.

A cake?

People were smiling. Gladys Kravitz caught sight of the cake and looked surprised, then embarrassed, then grateful.

"Wait," I said, confused. "What's going on?"

We kept watching. People were laughing now, including Gladys Kravitz. At some point, Happy Pants had transferred the flowers into a vase, which she now presented to Gladys Kravitz.

A party. That's what was going on. Maybe it was a birthday party, or maybe Gladys Kravitz was leaving the bank, and the others were giving her a little bon voyage. That was the reason the teller hadn't wanted to let Golden Girl into her safe-deposit box—and why Happy Pants had been watching them so closely: They didn't want to delay the party. The flowers were just flowers, and if that cell phone call a day earlier had been anything at all, it had probably just been her ordering a cake.

Boy, did I feel stupid.

Victor and Curtis didn't say anything, but I could tell they felt just as stupid. We had *all* jumped to conclusions.

"Curtis," I said. "I'm sorry. It wasn't a bad idea. Honestly." After a disappointment like that, there was no way I was going to dump on him.

Even Victor wasn't rubbing it in. "I bet those robberies really *were* an inside job," he said.

Curtis looked almost catatonic. "We should go," he

whispered. "We've wasted enough time here already."

"Yeah," I said. But then I stopped. "Wait. No." I *really* had to pee. I'd been sitting at that table drinking ice water all day. "I'll be right back," I said.

I made my way down the hallway toward the restrooms in the back of the coffee shop. Suddenly I overheard voices from the kitchen.

"Well, they're up to *something*," a guy said. "They've been sitting there all afternoon. Can't you just tell them to leave?"

"Sure, I *could*," said a woman—the waitress. "But it's better if they go on their own. They're just about to leave, I think."

"Relax, Jerome," a third voice said. "They're harmless. They're—what? Fourteen years old?"

Fifteen! I wanted to shout. Was this person *blind*?

I didn't want the people in the kitchen to know I was eavesdropping, but on the other hand, I still had to pee. As I crept down the hallway toward the restrooms, I saw over a swinging door into the kitchen. The waitress was talking to two men, a younger, skinny cook dressed in food-spattered white and a burly older guy with a leather jacket and a shaved head. The two men had their backs to me, and the waitress was standing in profile. Behind them, back between a set of shelves and the stainless steel refrigerator, a pair of binoculars hung on the wall.

"They're *probably* harmless," the waitress was saying. "But they are watching the bank."

"So?" said the guy with the shaved head, solid and unflinching. "So are we. That's the whole reason we're here."

"That's the *point*, Eddy," said the cook, as twitchy as the other guy was cool. "Do we really want anyone else knowing what a great place this is to watch the bank? What if someone puts two and two together?"

It took me a second, but then I got it.

These guys are the bank robbers!

I immediately ducked back into the hallway, away from the swinging door.

Curtis had been wrong when he'd thought the robberies were inside jobs; they didn't involve anyone from inside the bank. But they *did* involve the people from the coffee shop just across the street!

Talk about a robbery in plain sight! It was all so obvious. It also explained why it didn't matter that so few people ate in the restaurant. It was a setup to spy on the bank. In fact, fewer customers were probably *better* for them. They probably used those binoculars to peer into the bank's open vault.

I have to tell Curtis and Victor what I know! I thought. But to tell the truth, I also still desperately had to pee. *Do I have time to use the bathroom first?* I wondered.

No. This was too important to wait.

But just as I turned and started back toward our table, the waitress stepped out of the hallway into the dining room.

She looked over at me, then back at the hallway behind me and at the swinging door. I could see the wheels turning in her head. My only hope was to convince her that I'd been in the bathroom the whole time—that I hadn't heard anything that she and her coconspirators had been saying. I knew I could do it; I just had to be completely cool, absolutely unruffled. She thought I was only fourteen, so I was sure she wouldn't expect me to be able to lie convincingly.

"I was in the bathroom!" I said to the waitress, almost a shout. "I've been back there the whole time! I couldn't hear anything back there! Thanks for letting me use your bathroom!"

Okay, so even *I* wasn't dumb enough to think that she'd believe me.

I didn't wait for a response. I just stepped around the waitress and hurried back to the table. What was she going to do, *tackle* me?

"We have to go!" I said to Curtis and Victor. *"Now!"*

But I hadn't counted on the fact that the waitress might follow me. "What's the rush?" she said behind me, sweetly, her hand on my shoulder. "How about a piece of pie? You guys have been such regular customers, I'll make it on the house."

I stiffened. Curtis and Victor stared, bug-eyed, at me and the waitress. They could tell that something was up, but they had no idea what.

"Um, no, thanks," I said to the waitress. "We have to go to, uh, our jobs."

"We do?" Victor said. "What jobs?"

"Our *jobs*," I emphasized. "You know? Our *summer jobs*. My lifeguarding job? Your job at KFC?"

"Ahhh!" Curtis said, clueing in first. "Our *jobs*! Yeah, he's right. We have to go. We're already late!"

"Oh, honey, I insist," the waitress said. Unfortunately, she was holding a whole pie in one hand. She must have grabbed it from the case on her way to our table.

"Okay!" I said. "We'll wait here while you go get plates!"

"Just relax, sweetie," the waitress said, pulling up a chair. "I'll have Jerome bring us some." She looked right at me and talked to me like I was a puppy. "Sit."

I sat.

She began calmly slicing up the pie. "I think we have a problem."

"You're right," I said. "What's pie without ice cream? We'll wait while you go get some!"

She smiled—white teeth stark against her unnaturally tan skin. "That's not the problem. The problem is I think someone heard something he wasn't supposed to hear."

"*You!*" Curtis cried. "You're the bank robbers!"

"Holy Saint Lysol, Our Lady of Kitchen Grease!" Victor said.

I wasn't thrilled that Curtis and Victor had spilled the beans like that, but at least maybe the little old lady—the only other person in the restaurant—would hear them. She was done with her sandwich now and was standing by the cash register with her check. But she didn't seem

70

to have heard my friends' outbursts. She just kept calmly digging through her carpet bag of a purse for money to pay her bill.

"Not another *word*," the waitress said to us under her breath. "Jerome, honey?" she called back into the kitchen. "Would you get a check? I also need some pie plates and forks."

A moment later, the skinny, twitchy guy appeared from the kitchen. There was flour on his apron, and I wondered, *Could it be that the pie is actually homemade?* I thought he might be the waitress's son; they had the same eyes.

At the cash register, Jerome took the old lady's money. As she strolled toward the door, I frantically tried to catch her eye, but she ignored me. I wasn't surprised. We were teenagers. To most adults, we were completely invisible anyway.

"So," the waitress said when the old lady was gone. "What are we going to do about the three of you?"

"Let us go?" Victor suggested.

The waitress laughed. She'd served us all a slice of pie, but she was the only one who was eating. The pie was cherry, and the red juice stained her otherwise blinding teeth.

"We won't tell!" Curtis said. "We won't say a word to anyone."

I thought to myself, *If there was ever a time for Curtis to be a good liar, let it be now!*

The waitress looked over at Jerome. "What do you think?"

"I think," Jerome said as he bolted the front doors of the coffee shop and turned the closed sign face out, "that we have a very serious problem."

He wasn't twitching anymore.

It was only after they'd led us into the kitchen that I remembered from television how you're never supposed to go where criminals tell you to go, especially if it's somewhere hidden from sight.

"Where's Eddy?" said the waitress to Jerome.

"Gone," Jerome said. "He went to get us some decent food."

I looked around the kitchen. Any other time, it would have looked like an ordinary, harmless restaurant kitchen—except for the binoculars. But now, having been kidnapped by a cabal of bank robbers, I found it had a shockingly sinister appearance. For example, a magnetic bar along the wall held a row of grimy knives, including a thick-handled meat cleaver. Meanwhile, the grill sizzled, and the deep-fat fryer churned and hissed menacingly. And don't get me started on the *blender*.

Curtis was obviously seeing the same disquieting items that I was. But unlike me, he had a plan. Suddenly he reached forward and snatched something off the metal island in the middle of the kitchen.

"Defend yourself!" he said to Victor and me.

Prodded into action, we reached forward and grabbed the first objects we touched. When I looked down, I saw I was holding a plastic colander.

I looked over at Curtis and Victor; Curtis was wielding a metal flour sifter, and Victor brandished a plastic turkey baster.

Okay, this was too funny; in a kitchen full of knives and forks and mallets, we'd grabbed *these*? Somehow it just figured.

The waitress found this hilarious too. "Oh, no, they're going to *sift* us!" she said, laughing. "Would you boys *relax*? We're not going to kill you. Jerome and I obviously can't stay here. But we can't have you calling the cops on us either. So we'll be taking one of you with us. As long as the other two of you don't say a word to anyone for, say, four hours, he'll be just fine."

I immediately knew what television would say about a situation like this: Whichever one of us went with them was dead. After four hours in the car with them, he'd know too much; they'd have to kill him.

The waitress looked right at us and smiled. She still had cherry pie staining her white teeth.

"Well?" she said. "Which of you is going to come with us?"

How could anyone ask someone to make a decision like that? It was *crazy*, having to decide between your own safety and that of your two best friends.

Which is why I was so touched when all three of us said, at exactly the same time, "Take me."

Do I have great friends or what? I couldn't remember ever feeling closer to them. I was also very glad I'd spoken up; I could only imagine how embarrassing it would've been if I'd been the only one who hadn't.

A distant siren cut through the sound of rush-hour traffic outside the restaurant.

"What's that?" Jerome said.

"Nothing," the waitress said. "Just a passing police car."

"But it sounds like it's getting *closer!*" Jerome said.

It *did* sound like that siren was getting closer. Might I have been wrong about the old lady with the BLT? Could she have called the police after all?

"It's nothing!" the waitress said. "Let's just—"

"*Run!*" Curtis said to Victor and me. Taking advantage of the fact that the waitress and Jerome were distracted, he threw the sifter full of flour right at their faces. A huge white cloud exploded around them.

Victor, meanwhile, jabbed the turkey baster into the deep-fat frier, sucked up some of the boiling oil, and squirted it at the two of them.

"*OWWW!*" said Jerome from inside the billowing cloud of flour.

Wow, maybe the things we'd grabbed weren't completely worthless after all!

I looked down at my plastic colander.

Nope. Still worthless.

But I could still run. I threw the colander at the cook and the waitress, then lunged for the back door with

Curtis and Victor right behind me.

Once outside, Victor said, "Where do we go?"

"This way!" I said, running down the back alley toward a nearby vacant lot.

"Good idea!" Curtis said as we ran. "We can hide in the woods!"

I didn't say what I was thinking, which was, *Who cares about hiding in the woods? I just want a place where I can finally pee!*

Once we were sure the coast was clear, we returned to the scene of the crime. Police cars jammed the parking lot, their lights throbbing red and blue.

"Look," Victor said, pointing to the back of one of the police cars. The waitress and Jerome, handcuffed and downcast, slumped against the backseat.

"Ha!" Curtis said. "They caught 'em!"

A cluster of police officers surrounded the old lady from the restaurant.

"It *was* her!" I said. "She was pretending she didn't hear what was going on, but she really did!"

"This means, of course, that we'll have to split the

reward money," Victor said.

"Four ways!" Curtis said. "That's still seventy-five thousand dollars!"

We practically threw ourselves at the cops and the lady.

"Can I help you boys?" one of the officers said, stopping us.

"It's okay!" Curtis said. "We're with her!"

The police all turned to the little old lady.

She took a good long look at us. Then her face wrinkled. "Yes?" she said innocently, a little bit frail.

"It's us!" Curtis said brightly. "From the restaurant? You overheard us talking to the bank robbers?"

"I did?" she said, sounding confused, with just a touch of sadness. "That's funny. I thought I was alone in that restaurant."

Curtis, Victor, and I didn't quite know what to say to that.

"It's *us*," Curtis repeated. "We're the ones who solved the bank robbery!"

"Oh?" Her eyes dimmed. Now she sounded sad *and* tired. "I'm so sorry. I don't know what you're talking about." She swooned a little, leaning on one of the police officers for support.

"Okay, boys," the police officer said. "Move along."

"But—*wait!*" Curtis said. "What about our reward?"

"Reward?" we heard the old woman say, even as the police were leading us away. "I didn't know anything about a *reward.*"

Seventy-six-year-old woman solves bank robberies over dinner, read the headline in the newspaper the next day. Victor had brought it with him to the bomb shelter.

"'Mildred Shelby has never been one to eavesdrop on other people,'" he read in a shell-shocked monotone. "'But when the University Place resident overheard the proprietors of the Sunset Grill on Bridgeport Avenue talking about their involvement in a series of unsolved robberies of the Capitol American Bank branch just across the street, Shelby felt she had no choice but to go to the police.'"

"I don't believe it," Curtis said. "She totally lied!"

"Keep reading," I said.

"'It was a good thing she did,'" Victor read on. "'The proprietors of that coffee shop, Rene Blunt, forty-three, and her son, Jerome Blunt, twenty-five, were operating the business under aliases, and police say they were running it solely to observe the proceedings at the bank across the street. The pair has now been arrested in connection with Capitol American's string of unsolved robberies.'"

"Stop!" Curtis said. "I can't bear it! Just tell me if we're ever mentioned at all."

Victor read the rest of the article to himself.

"Not a word," he said at last.

"I can't believe it!" Curtis said. "*We* solve the bank robberies, and *she* gets the credit—and the reward! It's an outright robbery!"

There were two upsides to everything that had happened. First, there was the fact that none of us had been killed by the waitress and the cook. This was kind of a big deal. Second, there was the fact that we had learned just how far we would go for one another—that when given a chance to sacrifice it all, we would do it.

You might think that would have been enough to make us happy, to get us over the sting of losing that hundred-thousand-dollar reward.

You might think that. But it wasn't.

WEEK 4:

Counting Beans
(And Not Spilling Them)

That thing with the bank never happened.

It was one thing to make almost six thousand dollars by selling your most prized possessions in a garage sale and then lose it all in a fluke accident at the very end of the day. It was something else entirely to earn a hundred-thousand-dollar reward for solving the mystery of a bank robbery, only to then have the money stolen by a conniving old biddy with a complete lack of conscience and a taste for bacon, lettuce, and tomato sandwiches.

It was just too horrible to contemplate. So we didn't

contemplate it. For the rest of the week, not one mention of the bank was made. We all just pretended it had never happened.

But before long, we had other problems. The next Monday, Victor shuffled into the bomb shelter and said, "My family wants to stop by where I work. My mom wants to meet the manager, and my little brother wants to see the refrigerator full of chicken."

Curtis and I looked up from where we'd been sitting on the bare floor playing Boggle with a cracked board we'd fished out of the neighbors' trash.

"Piece-o-cake!" Curtis said. "Tell them your boss strongly discourages family visitors. Say that if anyone stops by, you'll get in big, big trouble."

"I did!" Victor said. "But my mom at least wants a phone number. She wants to be able to contact me at work." We'd explained our missing cell phones, gone since our disaster of a garage sale, by telling our parents we'd accidentally dropped them into water. Our parents had all punished our "irresponsibility" by pointedly not replacing them, which was just as well, since we wouldn't have been able to afford the plans for them

81

without our allowances, anyway.

"Just tell her you can't take personal calls at work," Curtis said.

"I *did*!" Victor said. "She said that was ridiculous— that she needed a phone number in case of emergencies. If I don't give her one, she'll just look it up. Saint Verizon, we're screwed!"

"No, we're not," Curtis said. "Just set up one of those cheap voicemail services and give them *that* phone number."

"With what money?"

"Okay, okay!" Curtis said. "*I'll* set up a voicemail service. One for each of us. I'll use my birthday money. I think they're about ten dollars each."

"By the way," Victor said, somewhat mollified, "I also have an idea for Project Sweet Life."

We looked at him.

"Guessing the number of jelly beans in a jar," he said.

This was a new one. "Tell me more," I said.

"I was over at the mall," Victor went on. "They're doing this big promotion where you have to guess the number of jelly beans in a big glass jar. Whoever guesses closest to the actual number wins ten thousand dollars."

That last part sure got Curtis's attention. "That's *it*!" he said, leaping to his feet. "Let's get to the mall!"

"Hold on, Eager Edgar," I said. "Every person in town is going to try to guess the beans in that jar. What makes you think we'll have any shot at the right answer?"

"Well, sure," Curtis said. "With an attitude like *that*."

I rolled my eyes. "Attitude doesn't have anything to do with it. Either you guess right or you don't. But it's still just a guess."

"Not necessarily," Victor said quietly.

Curtis and I looked at him again.

"What?" I said.

"Ours won't be a guess," Victor said. "We'll *know* the answer."

But when we asked him to elaborate, he just smiled a mysterious little smile and said he'd tell us more when we got to the mall.

The place was mobbed. It was now the third week in July, and what were people doing with their summer? Gathering together to enjoy the weather and the company of friends and family? Reflecting on the meaning of the Fourth of July earlier that month?

Nah, they were shopping like rabid zombies at the dawn of the dead. They were fumbling through the clothes racks at Macy's, slurping down overpriced smoothies from Yogurtland, and lurching off with glassware and towering vases from Planet Warehouse.

We found the jelly-bean display under a big glass cube in the main entryway to the mall. The jar itself was at least four feet tall, corked and completely filled with colored jelly beans. It rested on a small podium, and a collection of decorative moneybags—small white sacks marked with dollar signs—had been piled around the base. To one side was a small treasure chest spilling forth fake gold coins, and on the other side was a stack of fake gold bars. Behind it all was a cardboard rainbow arcing down into a pot of more gold.

As displays go, it was overkill—too much stuff packed too closely together. But it had definitely attracted a crowd. People were staring in at the jar with eyes squinted and fingers pointed, whispering to themselves, trying to count the thousands of jelly beans. Others were busy scratching their guesses on little slips of paper, then stuffing them into the big box covered with dollar-bill wrapping paper.

Curtis went over to read the contest rules, which were posted on a stand near the display.

"What did you mean when you said that we wouldn't be guessing?" I asked Victor.

"We won't be," he said. "We'll *know* the right number of jelly beans. I think so, anyway."

"How?" I said.

"It's really a very simple math equation."

Curtis returned. "Bad news," he said. "Since we're under eighteen, we'll need our parents' permission to collect the money."

"I bet if we ask Dave's Uncle Brad, he'll let us use his name," Victor said.

"Only one guess per household," Curtis went on.

"We'll only *need* one guess," Victor said.

"They're accepting entries up until Wednesday night and announcing the winner on Saturday morning," Curtis said.

"Oh, we'll definitely know by then," Victor said. He was growing more confident by the minute.

"*How?*" I said. "You say we won't be guessing, that it's just a simple math equation. But how exactly are we going to *know* the right number of jelly beans?"

Victor leaned in close to Curtis and me. "It's a question of volume. We just calculate the capacity of the jar, then divide it by the space occupied by a single jelly bean."

"But we *can't* measure the jar," I pointed out. "It's behind glass."

"Correct," Victor said. "But we *can* measure a single jelly bean. We can buy some right here at the mall, at the candy shop. With that jelly bean as a reference point, I can then write a simple computer program that will calculate the volume of the entire jar, which I'll then divide by the size of the jelly bean. That should tell us almost exactly how many jelly beans are inside the jar. We just need to take a picture of the jar."

"Ah," I said. "But you sold your digital camera in our garage sale two weeks ago, right?"

"Right," he said. But then he smiled again. "Which is why I borrowed my mom's." He patted a lump in his pocket. "Cover me."

As we were leaving, we ran into two girls we knew from school, Lani Taito and Haleigh Gilder. Victor has had a thing for Lani since about the sixth grade; he can barely get a word out whenever she's around. It's pretty clear she has a crush on him too, because she whispers around him despite the fact that she's not a particularly shy person. But even though they are both totally hot for each other, neither one of them has ever done anything about it. They'll go on like this, I am certain, until their senior year, when they'll finally get together the night of the graduation party. Then they'll stay up till morning, talking about how stupid it was that it took them so long to get together.

Curtis, meanwhile, has his own weird relationship with Haleigh. For one thing, he always kicks into slacker mode around her, even though he usually has energy to burn. They tend to insult each other too, in a way that you just know means they like each other. Truthfully, I'm not sure what the exact history is between the two of them—if they've ever gotten together—because Curtis is not one to talk about his love life.

"Hey, Victor," Lani whispered.

Victor made an inaudible gurgle.

"Boy, they'll let anyone in the mall these days, won't they?" Curtis said, suddenly slouching.

"So says the himbo in the stained T-shirt," Haleigh responded. "What'd you do, finger-paint in that thing?"

"Look who's talking," Curtis said. "Uh . . ." But he couldn't think of another insult. Haleigh is the only person I've ever known who can out-talk Curtis.

This was crazy. We didn't have time for all this romantic subtext—we had jelly beans to count. And let's face it, there was still the very real danger of running into one of our family members at the mall; Curtis's older sister practically *lived* there. (It's also possible I was jealous. Victor had his whole awkward thing with Lani, and Curtis had his thing with Haleigh. But I had nothing.)

Which was why I was more than happy to stop this little lovefest before it even got started.

"Hey, Haleigh. Hey, Lani," I said, pulling Curtis and Victor away. "Nice to see you, but we were just on our way to do something really important."

They all looked at me with their mouths wide open, like they'd been just about to say something—all except poor Victor, who still couldn't get a single word out in front of Lani.

* * *

"Thirty-seven thousand, five hundred seventy-two," Victor announced.

"That's the number of jelly beans?" I said.

"No," Victor said. "It's the number of stars visible from North America with the naked eye. Yes, it's the number of jelly beans!"

It was the following day, Tuesday, and Victor had finally written and run his computer program. So after checking with my Uncle Brad that we could use his name, we biked our way back to the mall to drop off our answer.

"You really think that's the *exact* answer?" I said after we'd slipped it into the box.

"Well, maybe not down to the last jelly bean," Victor said. "But I'm sure we're within fifty jelly beans. And if we're that close, I'm sure we'll win. The odds that anyone would be any closer than that by sheer chance are astronomical."

"I can't believe you don't have a sunburn," my dad said to me that night over dinner. "All that time you're spending out in the sun?"

"Sunblock," I said, digging into my mom's chicken-Tater Tot casserole. "I'm using it religiously."

"Thatta boy!" my dad said. "Good for you. Don't want to take any chances with that."

Questions from my parents about my "job" were still making me uneasy. But Curtis had been right that fooling our dads hadn't been that hard after all. So much for my dad's surveyor's sense. True, we'd all had to write up regular "schedules" and keep to them more or less, but the truth was that since most people are so busy with their own lives, they don't really pay much attention to the lives of those around them. And while it had taken some pleading, even Victor had finally gotten his mom to agree not to stop by the KFC. Now if the money from the jelly-bean contest came through on Saturday as expected, all this lying would be totally worth it.

Then my dad said, "I should stop by for a swim."

I choked on a Tater Tot.

"What?" I said, and took a swig of milk.

"Your pool," he said. "I should stop by for a swim. I think I will. I want to meet your boss and your coworkers. After all, you are who you surround yourself with."

You are who you surround yourself with. If it wasn't clear by now, my dad took this theory of his very seriously. He once even dumped one of his oldest friends when my dad found out he was having an affair.

"Um, you can't come to the pool," I said to my dad. Technically, Fircrest was a municipal pool, not a private club, so there was no reason why he couldn't come. But I quickly told him what Curtis had told Victor to tell his family, about how our bosses supposedly strongly discouraged family visitors.

My dad dabbed his mouth with his napkin. "All right, I won't tell anyone who I am. But I still want to *see* them. When is your next evening shift?"

"Uh," I said, "tomorrow." I didn't really work tomorrow night, of course, but according to my fake schedule I did.

"Then I'll see you then."

"But—" Was there anything I could possibly say to keep him from coming to the pool? Not if I wanted to keep his surveyor's sense from tingling.

"What?" my dad said.

"Nothing," I said, wearing my bravest face. "I guess I'll see you tomorrow night."

"This is not a problem," Curtis said to me later that night. I'd told him and Victor what my dad had said.

"How is this *not* a problem?" I said, outraged. "Tomorrow night my dad is going to go for a swim in order to see me working at my summer job as a lifeguard! Only I'm *not* a lifeguard, so he *won't* see me! It'll totally spill the beans!"

"No, it won't," Curtis said.

"What?"

"Your dad *will* see you. Working as a lifeguard, I mean."

"*How?*" I demanded.

"I won't know that," Curtis said, "until we go check out the pool where you supposedly work."

We rode our bikes to the Fircrest Pool, which was still open by the time we got there. When we peeked through the green plastic privacy weave in the chain-link fence, we saw a medium-size pool shaped like an *L*. There were two lifeguards on duty, both wearing red shorts and white T-shirts that read LIFEGUARD. One was lounging in the tall lifeguard's chair at the crook in the *L*, and the other was slowly walking back and forth along the other side of the pool. The building with the office and the locker rooms was directly opposite us.

"Oh, this is *good*," Curtis said, taking it all in. "This'll be a piece-o-cake."

"How do you figure?" I said.

"This is mostly a pool for kids! There isn't even a lap lane. So he can't swim laps or anything. He already agreed not to talk to your coworkers, right? So he'll just come in, see you in action, and leave."

"I still don't understand," I said. "I'm not really a lifeguard. How will he see me in action?"

"Leave that to me," Curtis said.

Great, I thought. *Now Curtis is getting all mysterious on me too!*

The next evening, I found myself standing nervously just outside the pool office in a white T-shirt and a pair of Victor's red shorts. My T-shirt didn't say LIFEGUARD, but according to Curtis, that didn't matter. He said if you got most of something right, people tended to fill in the rest of the details themselves.

Suddenly Curtis whirled around the corner. "Here

he comes!" Curtis said, ducking into the bushes.

There was a small metal sign just above my head that read OPEN SWIM. The lifeguards hung it out when the pool was open to the general public. We knew I couldn't be inside the pool office when my dad arrived, but this was the next best thing.

A moment later, my dad rounded the corner carrying a rolled-up towel. "Dave?" he said. "What are you doing out here?"

"Hi, Dad," I said, trying to act nonchalant. "We threw some guy out, so he came back and egged us. I'm just cleaning up the last of it."

"Teenagers," he said disdainfully, which I thought was interesting, since I hadn't mentioned anyone's age.

"I'll be out by the pool in a minute," I said.

He nodded. "Okay, I'll see you there." He ambled for the pool doors. Now I had to hope my dad would live up to his promise about not making any small talk about me to the off-duty lifeguard manning the cash register at the pool counter.

Inside the office, I heard my dad paying to enter. A second later, the door to the locker room squeaked.

He hadn't said anything.

"So far, so good," Curtis said. "Now on to part two." He stepped from the bushes, then ducked into the locker room after my dad.

I waited a few moments, then followed them both in. I paid my dollar admission, as had Curtis, then slipped inside the locker room.

"That's true, Mr. Landers," I overheard Curtis saying to my dad, "but we're all so busy with our summer jobs that we hardly ever see each other."

"There's nothing wrong with being busy," my dad said. "Being busy is a *good* thing."

"Oh, I couldn't agree more, sir," Curtis said, lying brazenly. "The harder I work mowing lawns at the golf course, the better it feels when I stop by here after work for a quick, refreshing dip in the pool."

In short, Curtis had pretended to accidentally run into my dad in the locker room and was now distracting him so that I could sneak past him, out into the pool area. That way when my dad went out to the pool and saw me, he'd think that I got there through the office, as I would have if I was really an employee.

I held my breath as I stole across the locker room.

"Yessir," Curtis was saying. "Nothing like hard work.

The harder, the better!"

Once in the pool area, I took in the scene. This late at night, there were only a handful of people in the water, with the two lifeguards in their usual positions. *You are who you surround yourself with,* I thought. Sure enough, the lifeguards looked well-groomed and attentive to their jobs. I was certain my dad would think they'd be great influences on me.

I waited until I heard the echo of Curtis coughing inside the locker room. That was the signal that my dad had changed into his suit and was now heading out for the pool.

I immediately veered for the tall lifeguard's chair. I stood at its base looking out at the kids splashing in the water.

"Wow," I said. "Not a lot of kids here tonight, are there?"

The lifeguard glanced down at me. "No," she said. "Nights are usually pretty slow."

"Must be nice for you guys. Not to have to deal with all those screaming kids."

The point, of course, wasn't *what* I said to that lifeguard. The point was that when my dad stepped out from that locker room, he would see me out there on the pool deck, wearing red shorts and a white T-shirt and studiously conferring with the similarly garbed lifeguard.

Which was exactly what happened. I could *feel* him watching me. But that was fine, because I looked like I was exactly where I was supposed to be.

"I'm sorry," the lifeguard said to me. "I'm not supposed to talk to people when I'm on duty like this. If you have a question, you can ask at the front office."

"Oh, I understand," I said, exaggerating a nod. "I definitely, totally understand."

This was an unexpected development. But fortunately, Curtis's plan did not require that I keep talking to this lifeguard for much longer.

Sure enough, at that exact moment, lightning flashed from somewhere beyond the chain-link fence. A second later, distant thunder rumbled.

A few moments later, it happened again.

It wasn't real lightning, of course. It was Victor, standing just behind the green plastic fence clicking the flash on his mom's digital camera against the big reflective sunshade from Curtis's dad's car, then wobbling, ever so slightly, a flattened aluminum roasting pan.

This had been my idea. In lifesaving class I'd learned that they had to close the pool for at least thirty minutes after any sign of lightning, since water is such a good conductor of electricity and no pool wants to be legally responsible for a bunch of deep-fried kiddies.

Sure enough, the lifeguard stood up and announced, "That's lightning, folks! Everyone out of the pool! And since we close at nine anyway, that means we're done for the day." I could hear the barely restrained glee in her voice about the fact that she was getting off work forty minutes early.

A chorus of disappointed groans welled up from the few remaining kids in the water.

The lifeguard, meanwhile, looked directly at my dad, who had still not gotten into the water. "We'll give you a refund at the front counter."

I looked over at my dad and shrugged helplessly. He rolled his eyes good-naturedly.

A few minutes later, I joined him in the locker room. "Sorry about that," I said. "You didn't get a chance to see me save anyone from drowning."

He gave me a proud smile. "I saw enough."

I nodded to the office area. "I've got to go put some stuff in the Dumpsters. I'll see you at home later, okay?"

"Sure thing," my dad said, turning to change back into his street clothes. "See you at home."

"It worked!" I said when I met Curtis and Victor in the bushes in front of the pool. "My dad bought it completely."

"What'd I tell you?" Curtis said. "Piece-o-cake!"

Even so, we waited until after my dad left so Curtis and I could go back and get our own dollar refunds from the pool office. After having spent thirty dollars on three voicemail services, we only had five dollars left between us, and we needed to keep every penny, at least until Saturday, when we were certain to win ten thousand dollars in the guess-the-number-of-jelly-beans-in-a-jar contest.

The announcement was scheduled for ten A.M., presumably so that all the people who'd come to see if they were the winner would then stay and shop at the mall. The winners weren't required to be present, but Uncle Brad and Uncle Danny had insisted on joining us.

It was quite a presentation. They had jugglers, a brass band, and a master of ceremonies who was dressed up like—who else?—Mr. Moneybags, the Monopoly character who just happened to be the Project Sweet Life mascot. It was clearly a sign!

"Just think," my uncle Brad said. "You guys might soon have *five thousand dollars* to split between the three of you."

"Ten thousand," Curtis said. "Not five thousand."

"Sure, ten thousand: five thousand for you three, and five thousand for Danny and me."

Uncle Danny whacked him on the chest. "That is *so* not funny." He looked at the three of us. "He's kidding. You guys did the work, so you guys get all the money."

"Shhhh," Uncle Brad said. "This is it."

"So you guys wanna know how many jelly beans are in this jar?" the MC shouted.

"Yes!" shouted the crowd.

"Are you *sure*?" Mr. Moneybags said.

"*Yes!*" responded the crowd.

He went on like this for about ten more pointless minutes, which seemed even longer since we were on constant lookout for Curtis's sister. But I reminded myself that once we won this stupid contest, we wouldn't have to set foot in public for the rest of the summer.

Finally, the MC announced, "The correct number of jelly beans is thirty-seven thousand, six hundred eleven!"

The crowd fell silent. They didn't know how to react. After all, the total jelly bean count was meaningless data to them. Most of them probably didn't even remember what they had guessed. They just wanted to know who had guessed closest to the total.

But the information was *not* meaningless to us. We did remember the number we had entered: thirty-seven thousand, five hundred seventy-two. Which happened to be a mere thirty-nine jelly beans from the total.

In other words, *we were within fifty jelly beans*! We had made the closest guess! The only way anyone could have *possibly* been any closer than us would be if they'd just happened to have made a completely random lucky guess—and what were the odds of *that*?

"It worked," Victor whispered, as if he'd surprised himself. "Saint Billicus Gates, we're rich!"

"And the winner," Mr. Moneybags went on, "the person who guessed closest to the *actual* total, is . . ." He paused dramatically.

Curtis, Victor, and I all had stupid smiles plastered on our faces. Even Uncle Brad and Uncle Danny grinned. They knew what our guess was too.

We'd done it! We'd actually done it!

"Lani Taito!" the MC finished.

Wait, I thought. *It didn't sound like the MC called either Uncle Brad or Uncle Danny.*

That stupid smile plastered on my face? Suddenly the plaster cracked, and the smile fell to the floor in little dry pieces.

I looked at Victor. The smile had crashed from his face too.

"No!" he said. "The odds of anyone making such a totally random guess—"

"It wasn't a guess at all," said Haleigh, stepping up behind us as Lani headed toward the MC, her mother in tow. "We had a plan."

"You did?" Victor said. "What was it? You used one jelly bean as a reference point to figure out the volume for the whole jar, right?"

Haleigh considered. "Interesting idea. Another possibility is to buy an exact replica of that jar and just . . . fill it up with jelly beans."

"But—?" Victor said. "How—?"

"Oh, it wasn't that hard to figure out," said Haleigh. "I mean, we guessed they bought that jar here at the mall. And sure enough, we found that exact same one over at Planet Warehouse."

What Haleigh had said made perfect sense. Why hadn't we thought of that?

If we had, we'd have ten thousand dollars!

But we hadn't, and so we didn't.

WEEK 5:

The Pirates' Plunder

Weirdly, I wasn't all that disappointed by our failure to win ten thousand dollars in the jelly-bean contest. Our guess had been remarkably accurate—it's just that someone else had been even *more* accurate. Yes, close only counts in horseshoes and hand grenades (and on Mrs. Stewart's biology tests, if you argue long enough). But our close guess, coupled with our resounding success at the fool-my-dad-at-the-Fircrest-Pool con, proved we were not incompetent, just that we were having a spot of bad luck.

However, Curtis and Victor weren't taking it nearly

as well. They spent the rest of the weekend kicking bottle caps and complaining about the unseasonably overcast skies.

Maybe they had more invested in the Project Sweet Life schemes so far because technically they'd been *their* ideas. Curtis had come up with the garage sale and the plan to catch the bank robbers, and it had been Victor's idea to guess the jelly beans.

Meanwhile, it was now the fourth week of July, and I hadn't come up with any ideas at all. That made me wonder if I was pulling my own weight. It also made me wonder if I wasn't a little dim.

So Sunday morning, I decided I was going to be the one to come up with our next project. And my idea, unlike the others, was going to be the one that would finally make us that seven thousand dollars.

But it's easier to *decide* to come up with a great idea than to actually come up with one. Short of finding buried treasure, how did one go about suddenly getting a huge amount of money?

As I was getting ready to leave the bomb shelter on Sunday night, I happened to spot *Trains and Totem Poles: A History of Tacoma, Washington*, the book that Curtis had bought at that estate sale. Maybe there was something in there, I thought—something about a lost treasure buried somewhere in the city.

Yeah, right.

I spent the next few days reading every word in that book. And wouldn't you know it? Tacoma just might have been home to a buried treasure after all.

"The China Tunnels!" I announced at the bomb shelter that Wednesday.

"The what?" Victor said. He still sounded grumpy, but I forgave him because we'd been sitting on a cold, bare floor for over two weeks now.

"The China Tunnels," I repeated. "That's how we're going to make the seven thousand dollars we need—plus a lot more."

Every kid in Tacoma knew all about the network of tunnels that supposedly ran under the city's downtown area. People said they'd been dug back in the nineteenth century when Tacoma was a major West Coast port. They got their name because Chinese laborers dug them, and because smugglers used them to carry Chinese opium and other contraband up from the waterfront shipyards to the bustling saloons and brothels along Pacific Avenue, the city's main street.

"Saint Ludicrous," Victor swore. "The China Tunnels don't really exist. They're an urban legend."

Wordlessly, I led them inside Curtis's house to their family computer. I quickly looked up Tacoma on Wikipedia. I scrolled down until I came to a paragraph that I'd found the night before.

Tacoma is also known, it read, *for having an extensive network of tunnels underneath its downtown streets. Referred to as the China Tunnels because they were once used to smuggle Chinese opium, these passageways are not open to the public, but have been explored and documented by urban tunnelers.*

"See?" I said. "It's *not* an urban legend!"

"It's Wikipedia," Victor said. "*Anyone* could have written that."

"True," I said, "but that also means anyone could have *corrected* it. And no one has! The author of *Trains and Totem Poles* talks all about the China Tunnels. He says there's all kinds of evidence that they really exist—old newspaper clippings that talk like they're real and WPA reports from the 1930s."

"That's cool," Curtis said. "But what does it have to do with Project Sweet Life? Finding the tunnels won't make us any money."

"Ah!" I said proudly. "Yes, it will! Remember the Calvin Labash coin robbery?"

Over a year earlier, right in the middle of the day, a masked thief had held up a rare-coin shop downtown. The owner of the shop, Calvin Labash, had activated a silent alarm, but by the time the police arrived, the thief had run off on foot, carrying hundreds of thousands of dollars in rare gold coins. The police followed but somehow lost him in an alley.

It was the perfect crime, except for one thing: Mr. Labash, who prided himself on his uncanny sense of smell, recognized the thief's cologne, an obscure European scent ironically called Bandit. Mr. Labash knew of only one person in the whole town who wore that scent: City Councilperson Ron Haft. The police questioned Mr. Haft, who even allowed them to search his home and downtown office. But when no evidence of the missing coins ever turned up, they dropped the case.

Mr. Labash, however, was *certain* that Mr. Haft had stolen his coins. He went to visit the councilperson.

Tempers flared, Mr. Labash pulled a gun, and Mr. Haft ended up dead. Calvin Labash was sentenced to life in prison for killing Ron Haft but committed suicide right after the verdict. Meanwhile, no one ever found his missing gold coins.

"What are you saying?" Curtis said to me. "You think the missing Labash coins are somewhere down in the China Tunnels?"

"Think about it," I said. "Mr. Haft stole the coins, then ran off *on foot*? Down an *alley*? The only way anyone would have done that would be if he *knew* he had the perfect getaway. And he did! There must be an entrance to the China Tunnels in that alley where he lost the police. He hid the coins somewhere down in the tunnels, thinking that he would return to collect them later. But he made a mistake in wearing the same cologne that he wore every day. Even so, he would have been fine, since the coins were still safely hidden, and there was no other evidence connecting him to the crime. I'm sure that's why he let the police search his home and office. But then Mr. Labash lost his head and killed Mr. Haft. So those gold coins are *still* down there. I can't believe no one ever thought of this at the time!"

"No one thought of it at the time," Victor said, "because the China Tunnels don't really exist."

"But if they *did* exist," I said, "who would be most likely to know about them? A city councilperson! He'd have access to city records. See how everything fits together?"

Curtis nodded. "It does make sense. It makes *perfect* sense! You thought of all this?" he asked me.

"Yup!" I said proudly.

I had impressed Curtis—but then he had a tendency to jump to conclusions. Victor still looked skeptical.

"Maybe it *is* a long shot," I said. "But catching the bank robbers was a long shot too, and we did it, even if we didn't get the reward."

"What robbers?" Victor said. "What bank?" Even now, he was still pretending like that thing with the bank had never happened.

"I'm in," Curtis said, just like I knew he would.

Victor sighed. "Okay. But let's start tomorrow. Today let's see about getting some new furniture for the bomb shelter. Sitting on this concrete is killing my butt."

★ ★ ★

One of the best things about a fictional job is that you can completely set your own hours. The hours I set for my "lifeguarding job" were afternoons and evenings. That meant that I could sleep in every day of the week, and there was nothing my parents could do about it (except grumble continuously and bang pots and pans in the kitchen during breakfast, proving once and for all that adults are not necessarily any more mature than the teenagers they criticize).

The next day, I met Curtis and Victor at eleven A.M. sharp. It's a long way from the suburbs to downtown, even farther than it is to the North End where Uncle Brad and Uncle Danny live. But with only five dollars left, we couldn't afford bus fare, so we rode our bikes.

A hundred years ago, downtown Tacoma had been a bustling place, the western terminus to the Northern Pacific Railroad, outshining even neighboring Seattle thirty miles to the north. But after that, it had been a long slow slide for the city. At its lowest point, which I guess came in the 1970s, downtown had basically been a wasteland of porn shops and abandoned buildings.

But lately, the area had been showing signs of life

again. New condos were going in everywhere, and the old buildings were being converted into offices, restaurants, and shops. There were museums and a big new convention center, even a light rail system that ran from one end of downtown to the other.

Even so, Curtis, Victor, and I didn't go downtown much. You know how cities are sometimes divided into parking zones—where you need a particular sticker on your car to park someplace for more than an hour or two? It's like downtown Tacoma has been zoned "adults only," and not just for cars. The YMCA, for example, doesn't allow anyone under sixteen. And even the Dungeon Door, a new gaming shop for Dungeons & Dragons and other role-playing geeks, had always made it clear that we weren't welcome, that they're only interested in *adult* gamers.

We stopped our bikes on the hill above downtown. Tacoma doesn't have skyscrapers exactly, but dingy bank buildings rose up from below like overturned cardboard boxes. Like San Francisco, the downtown was built on really steep hills. But unlike San Francisco, there are no cable cars to take you up and down.

I was wary. None of our immediate family members

worked downtown, but that didn't mean no one ever went there. We were supposed to be at our jobs right then, and all it would take for our whole plan to be exposed was one family member driving by in a car. It was funny how I kept telling myself we only needed to be seen in public "one more time"—but it never seemed to work out that way.

"Let's go," Curtis said, rolling forward on his bike. I think he also realized what sitting ducks we were on the downtown streets.

"Hold on, Indiana Jones," Victor said. "First, we need to stop by the library." The main branch of the Tacoma Library was just down the street.

"The *library?*" Curtis said. "Libraries are for wusses!"

"I want to see these newspaper clippings and WPA reports," Victor said. "They might give us some clues."

Victor had a good point; I wished I'd thought of it.

The downtown library has an entire room devoted to local history. It's located in the oldest, mustiest part of the building, under a big dome with peeling blue paint. The librarian was a fat man with fire-red hair and bad teeth.

"Excuse me," Victor said to the librarian. "We're

looking for information on the China Tunnels."

His eyes widened ever so slightly. Then he regarded us from head to toe (disapprovingly, natch).

"They don't exist," he said firmly. "It's an urban legend."

"Oh, we know *that*," Curtis said matter-of-factly. "But we're looking for information *about* the urban legend."

"What for?" the librarian said.

"School project," Curtis said, using his catchall lie, one I'd heard him tell a hundred times before.

"In July?"

This is exactly what I mean about downtown not being very welcoming to people our age.

"It's a *summer school* project," Curtis said. "Look, will you help us or not?"

The librarian sighed, but then he showed us how to use the computer archives that stored old newspaper articles.

Once the librarian left us alone, Curtis whispered, "He *knows* something! He was lying when he said the China Tunnels don't exist."

Victor rolled his eyes. "Obviously." He looked at me.

"Dave, I'm sorry about what I said before. You were right. The China Tunnels are real."

Most of the newspaper references to the China Tunnels seemed to involve buildings in the Old City Hall District. The Old City Hall is this big terra-cotta brick structure that was once city hall but has since been remodeled into lawyers' offices. The building was on the cover of *Trains and Totem Poles*, with a big clock tower and everything.

We locked our bikes at the top of the Spanish Steps, a set of white stairs that's a re-creation of a Roman landmark. The steps connect the upper streets of downtown with the lower Old City Hall District.

Many of the buildings we came across in our research are still standing. For example, 709 Pacific Avenue, once called the Bodega Bar, is now a place named Meconi's Pub. One of the articles mentioned something about an open entrance to the tunnels in the basement of this building, so that's where we went first.

Directly in front of the pub was a double row of purple sidewalk lights—small glass squares set in concrete to allow light into an area below. A few of the squares had been broken, so we crouched down to see what we could see.

Curtis peered through one of the holes. "There's definitely something down there," he said.

"It's too dark to see," Victor said. "It could just be a basement."

I poked my nose in one of the holes and took a whiff. "Smells pretty musty," I said.

We stood up, brushed ourselves off, and strolled in through the front door of Meconi's. The afternoon crowd was light. The air smelled like men's cologne and onion rings.

We'd barely gotten ten feet when the waitress said, "Sorry, boys! This is a pub. You have to be twenty-one to be in here."

"Oh!" Curtis said with practiced innocence. "Sure thing. But hey, do you mind if we use the bathroom real quick?" I especially liked the way he quivered a little and gestured to his crotch when he asked this, like he was a little kid who might not be able to hold it.

The waitress shrugged helplessly. "Sorry. It's *illegal*. Try the Indian restaurant down the street."

We had no choice but to turn and go.

A block or so away, we tried the Olympus Hotel, which was also rumored to have an entrance to the China Tunnels in its basement. It isn't a hotel anymore. Now it's low-income housing, but it still has dark wood paneling on the walls and a floor of small hexagon-shaped tiles, like those in the bathroom of an old train station. It also has a looming front desk, now partitioned behind glass. We hadn't even gotten five feet into the lobby when the man behind the counter said, "Can I help you boys with something?"

"We were wondering if we could have a look around the building," Curtis said. "It's for a school project."

"In July?" the clerk said.

"Summer school."

The clerk smiled. "Sorry. Can't leave the front desk."

Curtis hesitated a second, but I think even he knew he couldn't lie his way into this basement. Finally he just nodded and said, "Okay, thanks."

We walked to nearby Fireman's Park, located at the edge of downtown on a bluff above the waterfront. It's a narrow strip of a park that overlooks the tideflats, an ugly expanse of shipyards and heavy industrial plants that stretches out across the interior of Commencement Bay. Two office workers ate bagged lunches at the picnic table while a sleeping homeless man wheezed in the corner gazebo.

"What were we thinking?" Victor said. "That we were just going to be able to walk up to these buildings and say, 'Hey, you mind if we search for hidden entrances to secret tunnels in your basement?'"

"We could come back at night," Curtis said. "I bet these places would be easy to break into."

"I thought we agreed not to do anything illegal," I pointed out. "Besides, I don't want to ride all the way down here and then home again at night."

"Then what?" Victor said. "How do we get in?"

I stared up at this big totem pole at one end of the park. A sign said it was the world's tallest, but I'd read somewhere that this wasn't true.

"We need to find someone who knows something," I said.

"But who?" Victor asked.

I looked away from the totem pole and my eyes immediately fell upon a Chinese restaurant.

I smiled.

"I think," I said, "it's time for us to have lunch."

For the record, not all of Tacoma's early history was positive. In 1885, the city became infamous for forcibly evicting all its Chinese residents. An angry mob gathered up the entire Chinese community and forced them onto a train to Portland, Oregon. The next day, they burned Chinatown and the possessions of all those Chinese people, then pushed the remnants into the bay. The city's actions were so notorious that they become known as the "Tacoma Method" when other cities debated what to do with their own Chinese populations.

According to *Trains and Totem Poles*, it was all about the anti-immigrant attitudes of the times. People, including the editor of the Tacoma newspaper, argued that the Chinese were taking jobs from everyone else; the truth was, they were simply willing to do the jobs that everyone else refused to do. What happened in Tacoma was particularly notable because the angry mob had the support of the city government and was led by the mayor himself. Nice, huh?

Anyway, fast-forward to the present. Tacoma now has large Korean, Vietnamese, and Japanese communities. But unlike Portland, Oregon, to the south, which benefited from Tacoma's stupidity and ended up with a huge, thriving Chinatown, Tacoma still has very few Chinese-American residents (or Chinese restaurants). I guess when a city makes such a blatant show of bigotry, it takes a while for people to forgive and forget.

It was well after lunch hour, so the Paper Lantern, the Chinese restaurant I'd spotted, was mostly deserted. There was a little bowl by the cash register soliciting donations for the Chinese Reconciliation Project, which had been set up to create a memorial commemorating what had happened all those years ago.

The restaurant itself was run by an older Asian couple—a short man with a crew cut puttering around back in the kitchen, and a woman with her hair in a loose bun who seemed to do everything else. The seats were gold vinyl, and unlike the greasy spoon diner, they weren't sticky at all. Back in the kitchen, garlic sizzled delectably.

"Dave," Victor whispered to me as we took a table, "we can't *afford* lunch."

I ignored him. "We can't afford *not* to have lunch," I said. "Don't you see? If it's true that the China Tunnels were dug by the Chinese and used by Chinese smugglers, who would know better about them?"

"The owners of a Chinese restaurant?" Victor said. "Isn't that kind of racist?"

Right then, the woman stepped up to our table with menus. We ordered the only thing we could afford with the five dollars and change that we had between us: three cups of hot-and-sour soup.

We were now officially broke.

The woman just smiled and brought us a pot of hot tea.

When she came back a few minutes later with the soup, I said, "We were wondering if we could ask you a question."

Her smile reminded me of a small butterfly, gentle and elusive. But I wasn't going to say that to Victor for fear that he'd call me racist again.

"Do you know anything about the China Tunnels?" I asked the woman.

Her smile immediately fluttered away. I followed her eyes to the back of the restaurant. The cook was now watching us warily. Had he heard us from all the way back there?

"Please," I said quietly. "It's really important."

"It's for . . ." Curtis started to say, and I knew he was about to tell her that it was for a school project. But this time, something held his tongue. Instead, he just said, very quietly, "It's really important."

"I'm sorry," the woman said. "I can't help you."

She left, and Curtis whispered, "She *knows* something."

"*Obviously*," Victor said. "Do you think Dave and I are stupid or what?"

"But what can we do?" I said. "We can't *make* her talk."

We ate our soup. The woman never said another word to us the whole time.

Before we left, she gave us three fortune cookies. I felt guilty that she'd given us tea *and* cookies after we'd only ordered soup. The one person downtown who treated us like real people, and we hadn't been able to pay her back.

Outside the restaurant, I cracked open my cookie.

Sometimes the answer is right in front of your face, the fortune read. But someone had written on the fortune, crossing out *your* and writing *the*, and adding an *s* to the word *face*.

"That's funny," I said.

"What?" Curtis said.

And that's when I realized: *It's a message from the woman in the restaurant!*

"Nothing," I said casually. "Never mind." Careful not to show a reaction that might be seen by the man in the kitchen, I led Curtis and Victor back to Fireman's Park. Then I explained about the fortune.

"She wrote on the fortune *inside the cookie?*" Curtis said. "How is that even possible?"

I ignored him. "It's totally a clue! She's telling us how to find the China Tunnels, but she didn't want to come right out and say it. *The answer is right in front of the faces,*" I read aloud.

"But what does that *mean?*" Victor said.

"How did she get the fortune out in the first place?" Curtis said. "And then how did she get it back inside the cookie again?"

I kept ignoring Curtis. "Faces," I said, thinking

123

aloud. "What faces?"

Victor pointed over at the clock tower rising up from Old City Hall. "The clock tower?"

"But that has four faces," I said. "Each one facing in a different direction. That doesn't help us. I don't think that's what she meant."

"I just want to know how she got that fortune in and out of that cookie!" Curtis said.

"*Tweezers!*" I exploded. "Would you give it a *rest!*"

As I whirled away from him in annoyance, my eyes fell on the World's Largest Totem Pole, rising above Fireman's Park.

"Wait," I said. "That's *it!*"

The totem pole definitely had different faces—fifteen in all. It was hard to tell what most of the carvings were supposed to represent. There was a bear, a baby, something that looked sort of like a chipmunk, and something else that was maybe a frog. At the very top was an eagle with its wings extended, and perched on one of the wings was a real-life seagull.

All those faces, even the seagull's, were peering in the same direction: toward the opposite end of the park.

We followed the direction of the totem pole, walking the narrow park, but we didn't see a thing. Finally, we reached the far end. There was a colony of feral cats living in the undeveloped greenbelt that bordered the park, and three of them watched us, as if in fascination, from behind the protection of a waist-high chain-link fence.

"There's nothing here," I said. I pointed to one of the old brick structures nearby, now an architect's office. "Does she mean that building? There's a back entrance—maybe it's unlocked."

I started toward the door, walking across a little field of ground cover.

And something squeaked under my feet.

I looked down and tried to kick the foliage out of the way. Something squeaked again.

I was standing on an old metal grate.

"There's something here," I said. I crouched down, pushing the bushes aside, and peered through the iron. "And it leads *down*."

"It's probably just a sewer," Victor said. "That's all."

"It's *not* a sewer!" Curtis said. "Why would there be a sewer in a park? Is it locked?"

The grate wasn't locked, but it was very heavy. It took all three of us to lift it up.

I glanced over to see the feral cats watching us with wide eyes and bristled fur.

Curtis noticed the cats too. "It was the scrape of the metal," he said. "It sounded like an animal or something."

Without warning, all three cats bolted into the bushes at the same time. It wasn't just the scrape of the metal that had frightened them; it was something about the opening of the grate. But what did they have to be frightened about?

"They're *cats*," Curtis said, reading my mind. "You know how weird cats are."

"We'll need flashlights," Victor said.

I turned and dug into my backpack. Incredibly, I'd actually remembered to bring them.

A narrow shaft plunged down into darkness. A rusty metal ladder clung to walls of stone. The air smelled musty— not like sewage but like what we'd smelled through those broken sidewalk lights.

Curtis tested the top rung with his foot.

"It seems okay," he said.

We climbed down for what seemed like a long time. When we reached the bottom, we found ourselves in a cold cavern of ancient stone and stale dirt.

"It's real!" I whispered. "The China Tunnels are *real*."

"And if the tunnels really exist," Curtis said, his voice echoing, "I bet the Labash gold coins do too!"

We turned on the flashlights and saw that this was definitely no sewer. It was a tunnel lined with large gray stones. The roof was low and rounded, and the floor was packed dirt. I expected to see cobwebs, but there weren't any. The air was stale—at least ten degrees chillier than it had been aboveground. Victor brushed himself off, even though we hadn't touched anything yet.

It was also damp. This made sense since it rains a lot in Tacoma, and all the water from above had to go somewhere. You could taste the water in the air, along with the wet dirt.

"Now what?" I said. My voice echoed so cleanly, you could hear the quiver.

"Now we check it out!" Curtis said. Of course there

was no quiver in his echo.

Since the tunnel dead-ended behind us, we had no choice but to go forward.

Twenty feet ahead, the tunnel joined another that ran perpendicular to the first. The far wall changed from gray stone to blood-red brick. These definitely weren't modern bricks, fat and solid and cleanly shaped. No, they were long and narrow, and crumbling from age. Here it wasn't so much an actual tunnel but what seemed to be the space between the foundations of two buildings.

We turned right and continued on. A few feet later we saw another turn, even as the main tunnel kept going; it was an absolute maze down there. As we walked on, looking down offshoots and side passages, I noticed that almost every leg of the tunnel was different than the one before it. Most were lined with stone or brick, but sometimes the tunnels weren't tunnels at all, but forgotten cellars or crawl spaces that ran off from the main tunnel. And sometimes, the tunnels were just dirt shafts, like mine shafts, with ancient wooden struts supporting the ceiling. It was all completely makeshift and chaotic.

All the tunnels had in common was that they were very, very old. The stones in the ceiling were charred in places, maybe from the torches of the bootleggers and smugglers who had traveled these tunnels more than a hundred years earlier.

Our flashlight beams probed the way ahead of us. I couldn't help but think that finding a small valise of rare gold coins in this maze of tunnels wasn't going to be quite as easy as I'd thought. Still, we had nothing but time, especially now that we were underground, away from the dangerous eyes of our various family members.

Soon the walls turned to blackened terra-cotta brick, and the tunnel became a cavern of some sort: wider and taller. To our right loomed three sets of rusted metal bars with smaller rooms beyond them, like cells.

"It's a dungeon!" Curtis said, his voice suddenly sounding dull.

"No," I said, remembering, unlike Curtis, to keep my voice *down*. "A prison. I read about this in *Trains and Totem Poles*. We must be under Old City Hall. This must be some prison annex they sealed off decades ago."

But moving across the prison cavern, we came upon an impassable obstacle: a sinkhole in the middle of the floor. We aimed our flashlights down. The sinkhole was maybe eight feet across and at least fifteen feet deep, with crumbling dirt walls that would be impossible to climb.

"How do we get across?" Victor asked.

Curtis poked the light of his flashlight into the bars on our right. The doors to the first and third cells had been pried off, and the bars between the cells had been bent apart. Basically, others had bypassed the pit by working their way through the cells.

"This way," Curtis said, leading us into the first cell.

"Wait," I said, spotting something in the corner. "There's something in here."

It was the remnants of something white and powdery, like chalk. Most of it had been crushed into powder, as if someone had stepped on it.

"What is it?" Victor said.

"Looks like plaster of Paris," Curtis said.

"There are little drops of paint too," I said. "Black and white and tan."

"I guess some prisoner was doing an arts-and-crafts project, huh?" Curtis said.

"Not a prisoner," Victor said. "It's not nearly that old."

"Let's keep going," I said.

130

Soon we left the prison behind, and the tunnel turned to dirt again.

We didn't have a compass, but I was pretty sure we were heading north, burrowing right through a wooded hillside just above downtown. But suddenly the tunnel turned and ended in a rough rectangle of emerald light. Daylight spilled in through a thick curtain of hanging ivy.

I poked through the vegetation.

It was an exit from the China Tunnels—a hole dug in the wooded cliffside just north of downtown. It looked down onto the whizzing cars of Schuster Parkway, a concrete expressway built in the seventies, then to the train tracks below the road and a rocky beach below that. According to *Trains and Totem Poles*, the old Chinatown had been located just above that beach. If the Chinese really had dug these tunnels and used them for smuggling, it made sense that they'd have made an opening near their settlement.

"We need to go back," Curtis said.

"Back where?" I said. I was starting to feel a little claustrophobic, even if I wasn't about to mention this to Curtis and Victor.

"The Tacoma Municipal Building," Victor said. This was the current city hall building up above the Spanish Steps, where the local government had relocated to when they'd moved out of Old City Hall. "That's where the City Council has their offices, so maybe Councilman Haft came in and out of the tunnels through the basement. I say we head in that direction."

So back we went. But knowing the general direction we wanted to go wasn't the same as actually going in that direction. The tunnels, apparently created without thought or design, went where they went; our only choice was whether or not to follow. At one point, we passed under a set of purple sidewalk lights—maybe the same ones we'd peered down into in front of Meconi's Pub. Right then, it occurred to me that we weren't mapping as we went or leaving a trail to go back the way we had come. But it wasn't possible to get lost in the tunnels underneath a city—was it?

"Holy Labyrinthica, patron saint of brainteasers," Victor mumbled. "We could wander forever down here."

Right then, I happened to point my flashlight into a small alcove just off the main tunnel, and the glint of gold reflected back at me.

It wasn't just a valise of gold coins hidden on a shelf somewhere. It was a whole treasure *chamber* containing two big wooden chests spilling forth with shiny gold coins, strings of pearls, and jeweled necklaces—even a gold crown glittering with rubies and emeralds.

Needless to say, we were struck speechless. A lavish treasure was the last thing we had expected to find— especially one that looked like it had been arranged for a ride at Disneyland.

"What *is* this?" Victor said at last. "This can't be the Labash coins."

"Eu-flippin'-reka!" Curtis said. "We struck it *rich*! It's hidden treasure from Tacoma's early history! Pirates' plunder! Or a smuggler's loot that was stored here, then forgotten!"

Victor shook his head. "Looking this perfect? Right out in the open like this? And completely untouched for all these years? Remember, according to those articles at the library, a lot of people have been down here over the years."

"Yeah, well, somehow it happened!" Curtis said. "Because it's right *there*!"

What Victor had said made sense, but what Curtis was saying made even *more* sense, mostly because I wanted it to.

"But there's not even any *dust*," Victor said.

Victor definitely had a point. This treasure *shimmered*. What treasure would shimmer after being abandoned for a hundred years?

Victor stepped into the alcove and right up to one of the chests. He picked up a coin and examined it.

"Well?" I said.

Then he did something that made no sense whatsoever. He peeled the coin like the surface was made of foil and bit into something dark inside.

"*Victor!*" I said. "What do you think you're—?"

"Guys?" he said. "It's a chocolate coin. It's not real."

A chocolate coin?

The treasure wasn't real. The "coins" were all made of chocolate. And the crowns and jewels were probably plastic. Was that what that plaster and paint had been used for back in the prison underneath Old City Hall, to make fake treasure? But none of this looked like it was made out of plaster of Paris.

"Okay," Curtis said, "now I'm *really* confused. Would

someone please explain to me what is going on?"

"Kill 'em!" said a voice that echoed in from the main corridor. "Stick a knife in 'em and let 'em die!"

"That treasure is mine, I tell ya!" said another voice. *"Mine!"*

Even in the wan light of our flashlights, I watched the color drain from the faces of Curtis and Victor.

"Who?" I whispered.

"I don't know," Curtis whispered back. "But let's get out of here."

We hurried out into the main tunnel and back the way we had come. But almost immediately we arrived at an intersection.

"Which way did we come?" I said.

"That way!" Curtis and Victor said simultaneously, each pointing in a different direction. As for me, I would have guessed the third direction.

"We won't kill 'em just yet!" said one of the voices. "We'll round 'em up and make 'em talk!" The strange acoustics of the tunnels made it impossible to know from which of the four directions it was coming from.

"This way!" I said, making a decision and starting forward.

Almost immediately, we rounded a corner. At the far end of the corridor, a torch flickered, and in the light of that torch, I caught a glimpse of ruffled shirts, heads wrapped in bandannas, even what looked like a wooden peg leg. They almost looked like *pirates*.

Only one out of four chances that we'd pick the wrong way—and I'd picked it!

I immediately lurched backward, slamming into Curtis and Victor, who were following right behind. "Wrong way," I whispered.

I was pretty sure that whoever I'd seen hadn't seen me.

But *pirates*? Underneath downtown Tacoma? What was *that* about? Were they ghosts of the actual pirates who had left that treasure? But the "treasure" hadn't turned out to be treasure at all—just plastic and chocolate!

"Darn it!" muttered one of the voices behind us. "I missed my saving throw."

Curtis, Victor, and I ran back the way we'd come, past the treasure chamber and down an unfamiliar tunnel, turning blindly, then turning again. Our feeble flashlights barely reached ten feet ahead. It occurred to me that we could run straight into another sinkhole, but we were too frightened to slow down. At some point, I think we even went through an actual door.

Wait, I thought. *What was that about a "saving throw"?*

When the voices rumbled again, they were noticeably quieter than before. They definitely hadn't seen me, and they hadn't followed us, despite the clamor we'd made running through the tunnels.

When I finally took note of our surroundings, I realized that we weren't in the China Tunnels anymore. At some point, we had stepped into the basement of one of the downtown buildings, through a door that had been left open—a door that allowed access to the tunnels. Unlike the China Tunnels, the basement wasn't musty or dark; it was clean, paneled, and carpeted, with track lighting and plush furniture.

It was also full of treasure—but treasure of a different kind. On one wall, I saw two mounted staffs that I recognized as the ones wielded by the wizards Gandalf and Saruman in the *Lord of the Rings* movies; they had even been signed by Ian McKellen and Christopher Lee, the two actors who had played those characters. A nearby lighted glass case held clay miniatures from classic adventure movies like *Jason and the Argonauts* and *The*

Golden Voyage of Sinbad. In one corner, I even recognized the regeneration chamber of Seven of Nine from *Star Trek: Voyager*.

In other words, the room was full of *geek* treasures.

"Wait," I said. I tried to take in all the things around us. Then I glanced back in the direction of the pirates. "Something's going on down here."

"Well, then please explain it to me!" Curtis said.

"Don't you see?" I said. "Those aren't real pirates. They're people play-acting. *Role-playing*. They weren't chasing us at all."

"Holy Harryhausen!" Victor said suddenly. "The Dungeon Door!"

"I still don't—" But then Curtis clued in too.

We were standing in the basement of the Dungeon Door, the downtown gamers' store. Its owners had somehow found an access point to the China Tunnels. Maybe they'd rented the building knowing the entry to the tunnels was there. Or maybe they'd only discovered it after moving in. Either way, they were now taking full advantage by using the China Tunnels for real-life gaming. They'd even painted the access door so that it looked like a dungeon door, with wooden slats and a runelike inscription above it—SPEAK FRIEND AND ENTER, a reference from *The Lord of the Rings*.

What was all this? Some kind of exclusive gaming club where you had to pay a huge amount of money to get in? Or maybe they were just using the tunnels among themselves and their friends.

Suddenly I had a thought: Was *this* why they had chased us away those times we'd gone in to play—not because they didn't want teenagers, but because they didn't want any kids in the tunnels?

"Oh, no," Curtis said, pointing.

Hanging on one of the walls was a set of coins behind a polished wood frame.

Gold coins—*real* gold this time. Spanish doubloons, it looked like.

"The Labash coins!" Curtis said. He looked at me. "Dave, you were right—they *were* hidden in the China Tunnels! But the owners of the Dungeon Door already found them. It looks like there might have once been a real pirates' plunder after all."

"Hold *on*," Victor said. "We don't *know* these are the Labash coins."

"What else could they be?" Curtis said. "I mean,

it makes sense they'd find 'em if they've been down here gaming all this time."

Part of me agreed with Victor: We had no proof that these were the Labash coins. Curtis was totally jumping to conclusions again. But another part of me wanted to agree with Curtis anyway, especially since he was giving me so much credit for being right.

"And even if these *are* the coins," Victor said, "they don't do us much good. I mean, we can't steal them."

Victor was definitely right about this. We'd agreed Project Sweet Life wouldn't break any laws. Plus, it didn't seem very nice. After all, they'd found the coins fair and square.

Suddenly a voice called down from the top of a set of stairs. "You guys done already?" it said. "Seems like you just went down."

Curtis, Victor, and I hightailed it back into the tunnels and over to the exit in Fireman's Park.

Victor still wasn't convinced those were the actual Labash coins. So we went back the next day and searched more of the China Tunnels.

We saw some interesting stuff, but we didn't find any

more coins. And truthfully? Those tunnels looked like they'd been pretty well traveled. It made total sense that someone would have found the coins by now, at least if they were hidden anywhere obvious. In the end, even Victor agreed those Spanish doubloons on the wall must have been the Labash coins.

"So what do we do about the Dungeon Door?" I said that afternoon as we rode our bikes home. "What they're doing can't be legal. Do we turn them in?"

"Nah," Curtis said. "That's bad karma. If we turn 'em in, I'm sure the city'll just close off the tunnels for good, and what good is that? You gotta admit, they'd be an excellent place to game in. Plus, if we tell other people, it's only a matter of time until some stupid kid finds out about them and comes down here to explore and then falls into a sinkhole somewhere."

Needless to say, Curtis said this last part without any irony whatsoever.

WEEK 6:

The Perfect Crime

The following Monday I was eating a late breakfast of leftover Cap'n Crunch pancakes when my mom asked when I was leaving for work.

"Uh, I have the day off," I said. According to my "schedule," I didn't really have the day off. But I was getting tired of lying to my parents, and for some reason this lie-within-a-lie seemed somehow less serious.

As my mom was sorting through recipes, I noticed the front page of the newspaper. It had a big story: *Local woman receives reward for capturing bank robbers.*

Mildred Shelby, the article read, *the 76-year-old woman*

who provided the information leading to the July 11th arrest of two robbers of the University Place branch of Capitol American Bank, received her just reward yesterday—a check for one hundred thousand dollars, given by the bank's national headquarters, in accordance with a long-standing policy to thank those who thwart robberies.

It was the very end of July, almost three weeks after we'd solved the mystery of the bank robbers, and the lady who had taken the credit for it was finally getting her reward. There was even a photo of the old biddy smiling and accepting the check just outside the bank branch.

I brought the newspaper with me to the bomb shelter.

"She did it!" I said. "She finally got the reward money."

We were back to having furniture—a couple of folding chairs lifted from Curtis's garage and a lumpy, ratty couch that had been cast off by a house six blocks away and carried by us all the way to the bomb shelter just the day before.

"Who did it?" Victor said. "Who did what?"

I flung the newspaper at him. "Mrs. Shelby."

Victor didn't even glance at the newspaper. "Who's

that?" he said, sitting back against the couch. It squeaked like a dying pig.

"The woman who took credit for our solving the Capitol American bank robberies!" I said.

Curtis, on the other half of the couch, said, "Bank robberies? What bank robberies? I don't know anything about any bank robberies."

Even now, Curtis and Victor were still pretending the fiasco with the bank robbers had never happened.

"Look," I said, "you can ignore this all you want. But the fact is, *we* solved that bank robbery. *We're* the ones who put the pieces together, and *we're* the ones who almost got ourselves killed! Mrs. Shelby just happened to overhear us talking. Sure, she called the police, but anyone could have done that. And the only reason she got the reward was because she lied and didn't tell anyone what we did. That hundred-thousand-dollar reward is rightfully ours—and she's living *our* sweet life with it!"

Neither Curtis nor Victor said anything. They just sat there on the couch staring stubbornly in opposite directions. Meanwhile, I stared stubbornly at *them*.

Finally, Victor said, "I feel something."

Aha! I thought. I had finally lit a fire under Victor's

butt. Now maybe we'd *do* something about the fact that Mrs. Shelby had basically stolen our money.

Curtis looked over at Victor. "What do you feel?"

"I'm not sure," he said hesitantly. "But . . ."

Suddenly Victor leaped up off the couch, slapping himself on the chest and thighs.

Wow! I thought. I really had lit a fire under Victor's butt!

"Saint Pestilencia!" he swore. "This couch has *fleas!*"

"It does not," Curtis said. "A couch can't have—"

But then Curtis lurched up from the couch, shaking and scratching himself all over. Just watching them flail and jerk made me itch too.

"Do you think we'd have a couch with fleas if we'd gotten that reward money?" I said. "These fleas are Mrs. Shelby's fault! Those are *Mrs. Shelby's fleas!*" I didn't like hitting Curtis and Victor when they were down, but I figured I had a point.

Finally, when Curtis and Victor had slapped and shaken all the fleas off, Curtis reached for the newspaper article. He shook it for more fleas, then read it.

"That *is* our money," he said at last.

"I know!" I said.

"So let's go ask her for it," he went on.

I don't know what I had expected Curtis to say, but this wasn't it.

"For the money?" Victor said. "Oh, like *that's* really going to work."

"Why not?" Curtis said. "*She* knows she didn't really solve that bank robbery, and she knows that *we* did. So I say we go talk to her."

"And say what?" Victor said. "'Give us your hundred thousand dollars'?"

"No," Curtis said. "I know she wouldn't do that—and we don't need it all anyway. I say we ask her for seven thousand dollars. Just what we need for Project Sweet Life."

"It'll never work," Victor said. "We already know exactly what kind of person she is from the fact that she didn't speak up before. She won't give us a cent."

"So what?" I said, warming to Curtis's idea. "Even if she doesn't give us any money, at least we'll be able to confront her and say we know the truth."

Victor considered it.

"*Fleas*, Victor," Curtis said. "She has us sitting in a couch infested with fleas!"

At that, even Victor nodded. "Let's go see Mrs. Shelby."

It was easy to look up Mrs. Shelby's address online. She lived nearby, so we rode our bikes over there. The house was a modest two-story with a row of fish-scale shingles up in the gable and a flat-roofed carport rather than a garage off to one side. The sides of the front porch made up a wooden trellis on which a spindly-looking clematis grew.

We parked our bikes just outside the little picket fence and walked right up to the door.

It took her a long time to answer. The door creaked open, and the little old lady from the greasy spoon stared out at us. She had white hair and smelled of rosewater.

"Yes?" she said in her frail sweet-little-old-lady voice. She hadn't recognized us yet.

We didn't say a word, just looked at her.

She looked at us.

And then she smiled, an evil little twitch at the corner of her mouth. Her face changed too, right before our eyes. Her crow's feet suddenly got deeper, and her nose became more beaked.

Oh, she definitely recognized us!

"What do *you* want?" she said, but it wasn't a real question. It was a taunt.

"You know what we want," Curtis said evenly.

"No," she said. "I honestly have no idea."

"Money. Part of the reward. Not all of it. Just seven thousand dollars."

She kept looking at us.

We kept looking at her.

Then she laughed, an evil cackle.

"You're joking, right?" she said.

We were sort of taken aback, not by her words so much as the harshness of her laugh.

"We're not joking at all," Curtis said, recovering his cool. "You know what really happened that day. You know that reward money isn't really yours."

"Oh?"

"Please, Mrs. Shelby!" I said. "It's only fair."

She looked at me, and her face got very serious.

"In that case," she said, "let me give you something that is worth even more than seven thousand dollars."

This got all of our attention. "Yes?" I said.

"It's a piece of advice: The world ain't bloomin' *fair!*"

With that, she slammed the door in our faces.

None of us said anything for a second. Then I said, quietly, "Well, that was very frustrating."

"What a witch," Victor said. "You'd never know it by looking at her, but that woman is truly a witch."

"Forget it," I said. "Forget her. I'm sorry I even read that newspaper article. Let's go back to pretending that whole thing with the bank never happened."

But this time, we couldn't forget. The three of us barely said anything that afternoon, even when we rode our bikes over to Chambers Creek and hiked the greenbelt that ran alongside the stream. I knew we were all thinking about Mrs. Shelby and the hundred-thousand-dollar reward, even in the quiet cool of that pine-scented forest.

Sure enough, Curtis finally stopped on the trail and said, "I can't stop thinking about it!"

"Me too," Victor said.

"Me too," I said.

"That hundred thousand dollars is rightfully ours," Curtis said.

Victor and I both nodded. I had a notion that Curtis was going somewhere with this. But it didn't scare me like his ideas sometimes did. On the contrary, it excited me.

"So . . ." Curtis said. "Why shouldn't it *be* ours?"

Victor glanced at the forest around us, at the lush ferns and ripening salmonberry bushes. We were alone as could be.

"What are you saying?" Victor whispered. "That we should steal it from her?" But he didn't sound horrified like I might have expected.

"Not all of it," Curtis said quietly. "Let her keep most of her blood money. But what's to stop us from taking a small part of it? That's only fair, don't you think?"

It *did* seem only fair. She had basically stolen that money from us; how could it be wrong to take some of it back?

"How small a part?" Victor said.

"Oh, I'd say about the seven thousand dollars we asked her for," Curtis said. "Or something *worth* seven thousand dollars. That seems about right."

The moment Curtis said those words, time seemed to stop. Victor didn't twitch nervously like I would have expected him to, and even the birds in the trees seemed to stop singing. Seven thousand dollars did seem appropriate. But this was clearly illegal—something we had all agreed Project Sweet Life would never do. Still, while what we were planning was definitely illegal, it wasn't necessarily wrong.

Lost in the stillness of the forest, we stared wordlessly at one another. Why would we even consider doing this risky, illegal thing? I could tell that we all wanted to do it—maybe even *needed* to. But why? There was something none of us was saying, something we were all feeling but that we didn't fully understand yet.

At that point, all we knew for sure was that Mrs. Mildred Shelby had seven thousand dollars that was rightfully ours and that the three of us were going to get it from her by pulling off the perfect crime.

First, we needed to survey the scene. The next day, Tuesday, we rode back to Mrs. Shelby's neighborhood. We locked our bikes several blocks away and walked down her street to look around.

"That's it," Curtis whispered, pointing to a tree in a neighbor's yard.

We quickly scrambled halfway up the tree and carefully built something called a tree diaper. The branches of most fir trees are very elastic, and they grow in even rings around the trunk. You make a tree diaper, which is a kind of tree house, by taking a row of branches and bending them upward, then tying them off with rope to the base of the next ring of branches overhead. Once you've fastened the branches in place, you've created a sort of pouch around the trunk—a "diaper"—with a space inside that you can crawl up into. Assuming you picked a mid-size fir with lots of foliage, the tree diaper, buried within the other branches, is completely invisible from the ground, and no one can see whoever's inside. But once inside, you can see out fine. With the addition of a board or two to sit on, it makes the perfect viewing space.

"Three days," Curtis said. "Studies show that's the minimum amount of time it takes to get a sense of the rhythms and patterns of a person's life. If everything is mostly the same for three days, chances are high that it will be the same on the fourth day too, which is when we'll strike."

"Impressive," Victor said.

So for the next three days, my friends and I hid in that diaper, watching Mrs. Shelby's house.

We watched hummingbirds feed on her dahlias while her cat stalked bumblebees on the front lawn. We spotted two Frisbees, one red and one green, that had been lost on her roof. We saw how the postal carrier staggered under the weight of her daily mail, and how UPS never seemed to miss her house (for some reason, Mrs. Shelby got a lot of packages).

I admit I got bored after a while—so bored that I started spying on the rest of the neighborhood too. One woman did hair in her front room, for example, and there was a white plumber's van parked in front of the house across the street that had a Zone 1 parking sticker on its back fender.

No one could see us in that tree, including any passing family members, so we could finally relax for the first time in weeks. And I had my two best friends to keep me company.

At the end of those three days, we had learned absolutely everything we needed to know to pull off our crime. So, on the evening of that third day, we simply untied the branches of that tree and—*presto!* It was as if our perfect hiding place had never even existed.

The next day, we struck.

It was a perfect summer day. The clouds of July were

but a memory, and the stifling heat of mid-August had yet to arrive. It was late afternoon, and both the light and the breeze were as gentle as the butterflies that fluttered in Mrs. Shelby's flowers.

We didn't dress in black, and not just because we weren't going in at night.

"If we really want to be invisible to people," Curtis had said the night before, "we need to wear a uniform of some sort. Studies show that people see the uniform, but they never notice the person wearing it."

"Impressive," Victor had said.

So we'd all agreed to wear the same thing: navy shorts, blue short-sleeved shirts, and baseball caps. And *presto!* We were teenage window washers. Even though none of us had ever been fingerprinted, we made a point to wear yard gloves, since who knew when we *might* be fingerprinted?

Mrs. Shelby lived alone. Every day she went out for an early dinner. That's how she had ended up in that coffee shop in the first place, the day she'd stolen our reward money. Since she apparently ate alone too, her dinners only took about forty-five minutes.

"We should be in and out of her house in thirty

minutes just to be safe," Curtis had decided.

At 4:27, Mrs. Shelby left for dinner. That meant we had until 4:57 to pull off our heist.

At 4:30, once we were sure she had not forgotten her purse, we moved in.

Mrs. Shelby had a burglar alarm, which we knew she employed faithfully upon leaving her house.

"That means we can't enter through any of the downstairs windows," Curtis had said. "They'll all be hooked up to the burglar alarm. We could cut the window open with a glass-cutter, but I'd like to leave no evidence of the actual burglary. Studies show that when there's no evidence of a burglary—no broken windows or kicked-in doors—people wait much longer to call the police, either not noticing what was stolen or thinking that they must have somehow misplaced it."

"Impressive," Victor had said.

At 4:31, we entered the backyard. We'd brought an old metal ladder that we'd found that afternoon at Saint Vincent de Paul and had to carry more than a mile from the store; since we were still broke, we'd had to scrounge the four dollars for the ladder from under the seats of our families' cars.

155

We placed the ladder up to one of the second-story windows. We did not do this cautiously or in any way furtively. After all, we were dressed like window washers, and as long as we acted like window washers, we would be invisible to anyone who saw us—even to any of our moms or dads if they happened to drive by.

Or so Curtis said.

"Who's to say the second-story window won't be alarmed, too?" I had asked the night before.

"It won't be alarmed," Curtis had said. "Ninety-six percent of alarmed houses don't bother to alarm the upstairs windows. It's a way of cutting costs, and people assume, stupidly, that a ladder would be too obvious to the neighbors."

"But what if the window's locked?" I had said.

"It won't be," Curtis had said. "Eighty-two percent of houses leave their upstairs windows unlocked. That figure rises to ninety-four percent in the summer."

"*Very* impressive," Victor had said.

By 4:33, we found that the first upstairs window we checked was unlocked. We slid it open. Getting inside the window would be the one tricky part, since window washers did not usually crawl into the windows they are washing. But Mrs. Shelby's backyard was pretty secluded. We glanced around to make sure the coast was clear, then slithered inside.

You know what it's like to enter someone's house for the first time and smell its unique smell or see the way the light angles through the hallways? It's even more pronounced when you've *broken and entered* that house illegally. My senses felt incredibly heightened, able to distinguish between all the lesser smells: baby powder and rosewater and Ben-Gay and cat pee. Somewhere upstairs, a clock ticked. The glow of the afternoon sun suddenly seemed even softer, more yellow, almost sepia-tinged, and I wondered if it was because I was seeing it through rooms filled with glass kerosene lamps and lace doilies on antique dresser tops.

We're really here! I thought. *Someone else's house!* Suddenly Mrs. Shelby became real to me in a way that she hadn't been before—despite the fact that I'd just spent the last three days watching her every move. The inside of this house looked completely and totally different than it had from the outside.

"Wait," Victor said. "What are we going to steal?"

Why hadn't we thought about this? After all, it wasn't

very likely that she'd have seven thousand dollars in cash lying around.

"Let's see what she's got," Curtis whispered, leading us toward the stairs.

The hall floorboards creaked under our feet, a high-pitched whine. At one point, I glanced in at the master bedroom. There was an open jewelry box on the bureau, and I caught the glint of gold and gems—fake from the look of it all.

At 4:35, at the top of the stairs, I said, "Wait. What about a motion detector on the burglar alarm?"

"She won't have one," Curtis said. "She has a cat, remember?"

"I thought they made motion detectors that didn't detect pets," I said.

"They do," Curtis said. "But they work like total crap, so within six weeks, seventy-six percent of people either routinely bypass them or replace them completely."

Victor started to speak. "Impres—"

I interrupted him. "Yeah, yeah, impressive." I turned to Curtis. "Look, how do you know all this about burglar alarms and breaking into houses anyway? I mean, you even know statistics? Don't take this the wrong way, but you're not exactly known for spending all day with your head in a book."

"Oh," he said. "Well, I'm actually just making all this up as we go along."

"Wait," I said. "You're joking. Right?"

He shrugged guiltily. "Kinda not."

He turned to go, but I reached out and stopped him. "Wait. Really?"

He winked at me. "Really. It just goes to show that if you sound like you know what you're talking about, people will think you do."

It took me a second to process what Curtis had just told me. *He's just winging all this?* I thought. Behind me, I heard Victor wheezing, like he was choking on this new information. *Not so impressed now,* I wanted to say to him, *are you?*

"Don't worry," Curtis said calmly, starting down the stairs. "Everything I've said was just common sense. And hey, I've been right so far, right?"

"Saint Duplicitous," Victor muttered, but we had no choice but to follow. And in spite of everything Curtis had said, I still *wanted* to follow. There was something I *had* to do, or at least something I needed to know, even if

I still wasn't quite sure what that was.

Mrs. Shelby's stairs must have been built with a different kind of wood than the upstairs hallway, because they creaked in a totally different way—lower, more of a groan. The downstairs smells were different too: more dust, maybe from the ancient furniture, spoiled fruit from the kitchen, and the faint scent of perfumed soap.

At 4:37, we reached the bottom of the stairs and looked around. I don't know what I was expecting to see, but it definitely wasn't this.

The floor of the living room was covered with stuff.

Valuable stuff. There were computers and televisions and a Tiffany lamp and a crystal vase. There were bikes and a scooter and *two* game systems and other toys for kids. And on the dining room table, there was a gold watch, a cell phone, two pairs of diamond earrings, and a set of expensive-looking figurines from *The Wizard of Oz*. There was even more stuff we couldn't identify, things that had already been wrapped up as gifts in colored paper and bows.

Talk about the sweet life! I thought.

"What *is* all this?" I said.

"All those packages she was getting," Curtis said.

"Mrs. Shelby must be using the reward money to buy gifts. She's probably trying to buy back all the people she'd put off her whole life by being such a miserable witch."

This actually made sense. Mrs. Shelby had to know she wasn't going to live forever—so why not spend the money now? Now that I thought about it, the jewels in the box in her bedroom had probably been real after all—the part of her reward money that she'd spent on herself.

We kept staring at that stuff—all things purchased with the reward money that should rightfully have gone to us. There were any number of things we could take— things we could easily carry out the window and down the ladder—that were worth at least seven thousand dollars: most of the stuff on the dining room table, for example, or the jewels from upstairs.

But finally, Curtis said, "Okay. Let's go."

He turned to leave. He hadn't picked up any of Mrs. Shelby's loot, not even any of the easily pocketed stuff, like the jewels and figurines. Victor and I hadn't either.

That's when I knew. The perfect crime wasn't breaking into Mrs. Shelby's house to steal from her. The perfect crime was breaking into her house and *not* stealing.

This whole episode wasn't about getting the seven thousand dollars we needed for Project Sweet Life. It was about something else entirely. Mrs. Shelby had taken a hundred thousand dollars from us. We'd come to her house to prove once and for all that, unlike her, we *didn't* steal, even when we had the perfect opportunity.

In other words, we were proving to ourselves that we were *better* than she was. This is what I had felt before, but I hadn't been able to explain. It hadn't made sense until now, looking at all that stuff, having the opportunity to steal and deciding at that moment not to do it.

It made me proud to know that this was how all three of us saw the world—even Curtis. It was like that time in the coffee shop when we'd all offered to sacrifice ourselves for one another. I couldn't remember ever feeling so close to my two best friends. But now I felt even *closer*. I couldn't help but wonder if I'd ever feel this close to another person again. I wanted to believe I'd feel it on the day I got married, if I ever got married. But I honestly wasn't sure I would.

I glanced down at my watch. It was 4:39. There was still plenty of time to get out of the house.

As I was staring at my watch, a sound came from the back of the house—a sort of quick, soft squeal.

A squeal? Had Mrs. Shelby come home and seen our ladder up against the side of her house?

"It *can't* be her," I whispered, wanting it to be true. "She hasn't had time to eat dinner yet."

"It's *not* her," Curtis said. "We know she always parks in the carport, then comes in through the front door."

"But who else could it be?" Victor asked. It was too late in the day for it to be another delivery, and they'd all come to the front door anyway.

Whatever or whoever it was squealed again.

"It's the cat," I said. "That's all." But it didn't sound quite like a cat.

"No," Victor said. "It's someone really washing the windows."

I relaxed a little. Victor was right; it *did* sound like someone squeegeeing the windows. Sort of.

Something thumped against the ground just outside the back of the house.

That was no window being washed. Something was different *inside* the house: Dust motes whirled in the afternoon sun, and I felt a sudden draft on my skin, like a window had been opened. But how could anyone open a window without setting off the burglar alarm? I glanced over at the keypad on the wall and saw that, yes, it was still armed.

There was movement, the sound of a body coming through an open window. Feet scuffled on a windowsill, then water gurgled, like someone stepping on the top of a ceramic toilet tank.

Someone was coming in through Mrs. Shelby's bathroom window? But who? Another burglar? Maybe those squeals hadn't been someone washing the window, but rather, someone cutting *through* it. Hadn't Curtis said that was a way of getting inside a house without setting off the burglar alarm?

But another *burglar*? At the same time we'd chosen to break into the house? What were the odds of *that*?

Suddenly I remembered what Curtis had said about burglars observing a house for three days and then, if there was no change in the pattern, breaking in on the fourth. It had just been wild speculation on Curtis's part, but it definitely *sounded* true. So maybe it was. And today was the fourth day after that article in the newspaper about Mrs. Shelby getting a check for a hundred thousand dollars. It certainly made sense that the other burglar would strike at the same time we chose to, when Mrs. Shelby was off having dinner.

Then I remembered that plumber's van we'd seen in front of Mrs. Shelby's house for three days straight. What kind of plumbing job took three days to finish?

Someone else had been casing out Mrs. Shelby's house! And just like Curtis had had us disguise ourselves as window washers, this other burglar made himself invisible by dressing as a plumber. It had worked so effectively that even *we* hadn't noticed him!

Curtis, Victor, and I stared at the stairs in front of us. I knew what we were all thinking: Those stairs and the second-story floorboards squeaked. If we started up those stairs and someone came in through the back, they would hear us for sure. And since we would still need to climb down a ladder on the side of the house, they might very well catch us, too.

What did a burglar do when he or she ran into another burglar at the scene of a crime? Was there some kind of protocol, a way to call "dibs"? Or would he just kill us?

I didn't want to find out if there really was honor among thieves. On the other hand, we couldn't very well stay where we were.

"The kitchen!" Curtis whispered.

"The kitchen?" I whispered back.

"Just *do* it!"

We ran to the small pantry at the back of the kitchen. It smelled of dry pasta and molasses. I saw why Curtis had demanded that we come here: There was nothing valuable in a kitchen. It also had an exit.

The burglar was inside the house now, moving from the bathroom to the front hall. At one point, he briefly passed by the doorway into the kitchen. He didn't see us, but we saw him: an older, burly guy with a shaved head. Sure enough, he was dressed in a plumber's uniform.

He looked familiar.

The third bank robber!

How could I have forgotten? There were *three* thieves who had been involved in those robberies at Capitol American: the waitress, her son the cook, and an older guy in a leather jacket. He was probably the waitress's husband or boyfriend. I'd overheard them all talking back in the kitchen. But that third guy—"Eddy"—had gone out for food, and I'd forgotten all about him. I'd just assumed that the police had caught him too—even though the newspaper had specifically said they'd only caught *two* thieves. But how *could* the police have caught him? The newspaper said they'd rented the restaurant under aliases, and the waitress and her son sure weren't going to turn in their accomplice. And the informant, Mrs. Shelby, had never even known he existed in the first place!

I quickly whispered all this to Curtis and Victor.

"Eddy must have read about Mrs. Shelby and the reward money in the same newspaper article we saw," Victor said. "He probably figured he could make a fast score *and* get revenge for what she did to his girlfriend and son."

Out in the house, floorboards squeaked—first in the foyer and front hall, then up the steps and into the upstairs bedrooms.

"Let's go," Victor said. He nodded to the door in the pantry. "If we leave through here, it'll even set off the burglar alarm."

"Yeah," Curtis said, "but if the burglar alarm goes off, we might get caught too."

"What are you saying?" I said. "That we wait here until the burglar leaves and then go out the way we came in?"

"Why not?" Curtis said.

I looked down at my watch. It was 4:56—twenty-nine minutes since Mrs. Shelby had left and one minute until the time we'd intended to be gone. We'd been hiding in the pantry too long. Mrs. Shelby would be home for sure in just sixteen minutes. Inside the garden gloves, my hands sweated like crazy.

"I still say we go," Victor said. "The police won't be here right away, and we're fast runners. Let's risk it." He turned for Mrs. Shelby's back door.

"Hold on!" Curtis whispered. "He's leaving."

At first I didn't believe it. But as I listened, it *did* sound like the thief was working his way back to the bathroom, and back out the bathroom window. The toilet tank even gurgled again.

Once we were sure he was gone, we hurried out into the entry hall. I looked around. Some of the stuff was definitely gone—mostly the small items from the dining room table. I was certain the jewels from upstairs were missing too. Eddy had been shockingly efficient.

I glanced down at my watch. It was now 5:02.

"We need to get out of here," I said. "Now, before Mrs. Shelby comes home."

And of course that was the exact moment that we heard a key being inserted into the front door lock.

Mrs. Shelby!

She'd come home from dinner early! We'd been so distracted by the thief that we hadn't been listening for her car.

The door opened, and her burglar alarm started beeping—a warning that gave her a minute or so to turn the device off before it activated.

On the other side of that doorway, Mrs. Shelby looked right in at us.

It took a second for her to register what she was seeing. Then she said, *"You!"* An instant later, she glanced over at her piles of stuff and at the small but obvious gaps where expensive things used to be.

"No!" I shouted. "It wasn't us!"

"Don't bother," Curtis said to me. "Let's just get out of here."

Curtis was right: There was no way Mrs. Shelby wasn't going to blame us for stealing from her.

We turned and ran for the kitchen door.

And somehow we managed to get away.

* * *

We didn't bother calling the police. We knew there was no way they'd believe us, especially not after Mrs. Shelby had seen us inside her house. Fortunately she didn't know our names or anything else about us, so there wasn't much chance that the police would be able to track us down.

Still, something told me that the story about Mrs. Shelby and the Capitol American bank robbers wasn't quite finished yet.

WEEK 7:

A Deal with the Devils

"Fried chicken!" Victor said, bursting into the bomb shelter. "I need a bucket of fried chicken *now!*" Even without the crazed expression on his face, he would have struck both Curtis and me speechless.

"Wow," Curtis said at last. "That's a serious food craving." We'd gotten rid of the flea-infested couch, but that meant we were back to sitting on folding chairs.

"Not for *me!*" Victor said. "Someone told my mom that at the end of the day, the workers at KFC get to keep the leftover chicken for free. So she keeps asking me to bring home the chicken. I keep telling her that

171

there aren't any leftovers, but now she's starting to grow suspicious!"

I saw now why Victor was panicking; we were still totally broke, and fried chicken wasn't cheap. But this was just the latest of our problems. We were already seven weeks into summer, and the sweet life wasn't anywhere in sight. Plus, I was getting really, really tired of lying to my parents all the time.

"Okay," Curtis said to Victor, "we need some fast cash. How 'bout a car wash?"

Victor rolled his eyes. "We can't do a car wash. We can't do *anything* in public. Not only do we have to worry about our families seeing us, now we have to worry about Mrs. Shelby too! And if Mrs. Shelby sees us, we don't just get punished, we go to prison."

"Okay, okay!" Curtis said. "But we'll figure this out somehow. Trust me! Piece-o-cake."

So it all boiled down, once again, to trusting Curtis. What other choice did we have?

I looked over at Mr. Moneybags, who was still almost the only thing in the bomb shelter. With his outstretched arms, he made being a millionaire look so easy.

The truth was, it wasn't easy at all.

* * *

We got the money for Victor's fried chicken by fishing the change out of two bank fountains and a park wishing well. Needless to say, it was beyond humiliating. But Victor needed that fried chicken, and he needed it now.

That night over a dinner of fish-stick stew, my own situation became much more dire.

"So," my dad said to me. "Your bank statement came today."

"Wait," I said. "You opened my mail?"

"I opened it by accident. But I couldn't help but notice . . ."

I had a very bad feeling about this. "What?"

"Your balance is three dollars."

Whoops, I thought.

"So?" I said.

"So where's the money from your summer job? Dave, don't tell me you've spent it already!"

My life flashed before my eyes—including the time I saw college students skinny-dipping at Lake Chelan, which was a pleasant surprise both then and now.

Then, since my life really wasn't all that long yet, I tried to figure out how to deal with this new wrinkle.

I obviously couldn't tell my dad I was really unemployed. But if I lied and told him that I'd spent all the money I'd made, that would be almost as bad as if I admitted I didn't have a job at all. And it would just make him insist that I give *him* my next paycheck, only compounding the problem.

So I said, "No, I haven't spent it. I just haven't deposited any of my paychecks yet."

My dad stared at me, eyes narrowing; I think the surveyor in him was once again sensing that something wasn't right.

Finally, he just sighed and said, "Dave, Dave, Dave. That's not very responsible. Deposit them tomorrow. I want to see the deposit slip tomorrow night."

"Absolutely," I said, which meant I officially had twenty-four hours to live.

At that, my dad turned to my mom. "Did you hear they finally caught the kids who broke open the chimpanzee cage at the Woodland Park Zoo? Do you know what I'd do if one of them was *my* kid?"

When my dad isn't speaking directly to me, he has a habit of talking as if I'm not even in the room. In this case, however, it was a good thing, because he couldn't see how I was totally freaking out.

"What would you do?" my mom said to my dad, sipping on her glass of mandarin-kiwi juice blend.

"I'd split 'em up!" he said. "I'd make sure he never saw any of his hoodlum friends ever again."

My dad may not have been talking to me, but I was hearing him loud and clear.

"You said *what* to your dad?" Curtis said to me in the bomb shelter later that evening. I'd told him and Victor about how I'd promised my dad I'd have a deposit slip for him the following day.

"I didn't have any choice," I said. "It was either that or say I'd *spent* the money." I'd been in a bad mood since dinner.

"Don't be too hard on him," Victor said to Curtis. "Our dads must be talking again. My dad said he wanted to see my bank statement too. I told him I'd lost it, but he said I needed to get a new copy."

Curtis threw his hands up. "So we need to come up with—what? Fifteen hundred dollars for each of you? Three thousand dollars before dinner tomorrow night?"

"Better make it forty-five hundred," Victor said. "If

our dads are talking, it's a good bet that *your* dad is going to want to see evidence of money, too."

"There's more," I said.

"What 'more'?" Curtis said.

I told them my dad's theory about who you are being who you surround yourself with. I also repeated what he'd said over dinner about the boys who'd freed the chimpanzees.

"Oh, that's just talk," Curtis said. "He'd never really make you stop seeing your friends."

"He already did," I said. "Back when I was eight years old."

"What?" Victor said.

So I told Curtis and Victor something I'd never told anyone before, about a friend I'd once had named Shawn Kelsey-Emmerling. We met at soccer, and we didn't go to the same school, so we had to go to each other's houses to play. One afternoon, I'd gone to play at his house. He lived near a big train tunnel, and we decided to go inside even though we'd been told not to. His mom caught us and she told my dad, who was so mad that he said I could never go over to Shawn's again, that he didn't even want me to be friends with him anymore. My mom had tried to talk him out of it, but he'd just said, "You are who you surround yourself with, Colleen! *Our son* will be whomever he surrounds himself with!" Which just made me feel even worse about the whole thing because it had been more my idea than Shawn's to go into the train tunnel.

But my dad got his way. Sure, I still saw Shawn at soccer practice, but by then his parents were mad at my parents for blaming the whole thing on their son. Shawn and I were caught in the middle, and every time we spoke to each other, we had our parents glaring at us. So the friendship—my best friend at the time—just drifted away.

Even now, it made me really sad to think about Shawn Kelsey-Emmerling. It was the real reason I'd been in such a bad mood since dinner.

"Your dad wouldn't do something like that *now*," Curtis insisted. "You're fifteen years old! Besides, how could he break us up? We'd still see each other at school."

"Yes, he would," Victor said quietly. "And I think mine would too."

"What?" Curtis said. "No, he wouldn't—"

"I've heard the way my dad talks about your dad,"

Victor said to me. "He really looks up to him. He likes how uncompromising he is. And if your dad said we couldn't be friends anymore, I think my dad would back him up." Victor looked at Curtis. "And for the record, being best friends is about a lot more than just seeing each other at school."

Hearing Victor say this broke my heart. Curtis and Victor were really important to me, but I think Curtis and I might have been even more important to Victor. He wasn't the most popular kid at school. He'd never really fit in, even in his own family. They were loud and friendly and sort of simple, and he was quiet and bookish and complicated.

Curtis looked like he wanted to speak, but nothing came out. I think he was realizing that Victor and I were right about our dads splitting us up if they found out about Project Sweet Life—and maybe also that his dad would go along with them. It was funny how, even though I hadn't been nearly as certain as Curtis that the project would succeed, I'd never really thought about what would happen if we failed. Part of it was that at the beginning of summer, the end of summer had seemed a million years away.

Curtis sat upright. "Well," he said, "then we'll just need to make sure that our dads don't find out. How are we going to get the money we need by tomorrow?"

"Uncle Brad and Uncle Danny?" Victor said. He looked at me. "You could ask them for a loan."

I shook my head. "It was one thing to use their front porch for the sale or to have them loan us that two hundred dollars for the car repair. But this would mean asking them to outright lie to my parents. I can't put them in that position."

"Then who?" Victor said. "We don't know anyone else with that kind of money."

Suddenly Curtis's eyes lit up. "Wait!" he said. "Yes, we do!"

We met Lani Taito and Haleigh Gilder at the bottom of an abandoned gravel pit in a wooded area near our houses. Waterfalls of sand spilled down from crumbling walls. It smelled like pollen from the scotch broom above the rim. The tiniest sound echoed back and forth between the sides of this artificial canyon, making it seem like exactly the kind of place where spies would rendezvous. It was also a place where we didn't have to worry about being spotted by our parents. We'd called Lani and Haleigh and told them that we had something important we needed to discuss.

"What is it?" Haleigh said, getting right to the point. She looked even more self-satisfied than the cat that ate the canary; she looked like a canary that had eaten a cat. I wasn't surprised. She and Lani had to know we wanted something from them.

Victor made a soft gurgling sound. In the presence of Lani, he'd been struck speechless once again.

And to Haleigh, Curtis said, "Sorry we had to meet here, but we didn't want to be seen with you in public." Naturally, he'd kicked into slacker mode.

Good plan! I wanted to say to him. *When you're trying to get someone to do you a big favor, it's always best to start off with an insult.*

Being around Lani and Haleigh, my best friends had once again turned into complete imbeciles. It was up to me to handle this.

"Just ignore them," I said to Haleigh and Lani. "Remember when you guys won that ten thousand dollars from the jelly-beans-in-a-jar contest? Do you still have it?"

"Most of it," Haleigh said. "Why?"

"We were hoping we could borrow a little."

"A little?" she said suspiciously. "How little? And for how long?"

"Four thousand, five hundred dollars," I said. I figured there was no point in beating around the bush.

"*What?*" Haleigh said. "Are you out of your *minds*? We're not going to give you four thousand, five hundred dollars!"

"Not give!" I said. "Lend!" Now I wished I'd beaten around the bush.

"We're also not going to *lend* you four thousand, five hundred dollars," she said. "Do you think we're stupid?"

Curtis started to answer, but I interrupted. "This isn't how it sounds," I said to the girls. "We just need the money for twenty-four hours. Not even that long, really. We just all need bank statements to show our dads so it *looks* like we each have fifteen hundred dollars in our accounts. We could use the same fifteen hundred dollars three times. You can even come with us to the bank. We'll deposit the money, have statements printed, then withdraw the money and give it right back to you."

"Why do you need statements showing that you have fifteen hundred dollars in your bank accounts?" Lani said.

Being around Victor, she was whispering.

I looked at Curtis and Victor. I think we all knew that there was no way they were going to loan us the money without knowing about Project Sweet Life.

Curtis nodded, and Victor gurgled a little, as if to tell me, *Go ahead.*

I turned to the girls and told them everything.

"No *way!*" Haleigh said, laughing out loud.

Even Lani snorted.

I wasn't sure if they were laughing at us and the fact that we hadn't been able to earn the money or just laughing at the whole *idea* of Project Sweet Life.

"And here it is, the second week of August, and you *still* haven't earned anything?" Haleigh said. "Oh my God, that is so pathetic!"

Okay, so now I knew: The girls were laughing *at* us.

"Look!" Curtis said at last. "Are you going to help us or not?"

The girls stopped laughing, but they didn't stop smiling. They walked away and conferred quietly.

Finally, Haleigh turned and peered right at Curtis. "What's in it for *us?*" she said.

"Why should *anything* be in it for you?" Curtis said.

"Can't you just do someone a favor?"

"Oh, like if the situation were reversed, you guys would just do *us* a favor, right?" Haleigh said.

Even Curtis had to admit that she had a point.

"What do you want?" he said.

"I'm just saying," Haleigh said, "if we do something for you, you should do something for us."

"Yes!" I said, feeling desperate. "Anything!"

That sure got Haleigh's attention. "Anything?"

"Well, not necessarily *anything*," Curtis said. He threw me a look that said, *Thanks a lot!* "What do you *want* from us?"

The girls eyed each other again. There was something about their little smiles that made me nervous.

"We're not sure yet," Haleigh said. "But here's the deal. We'll loan you the money today, and then tomorrow you come back and agree to do whatever it is we tell you to do."

That was, of course, a ridiculous bargain. Only a fool would agree to it.

A fool, or someone who had no choice in the matter.

"We'll do *one* thing you say," Curtis said. "We're not agreeing to be your personal slaves all summer. If that's the case, we might as well get real summer jobs."

Haleigh shrugged. "Fine."

"And you can't make us do anything embarrassing," Curtis added.

Haleigh just smiled. "Well, I'm not so sure we can agree to *that*."

Once we'd settled on the deal, we all went to Victor's and my bank, which happened to be the branch of Capitol American where we had solved the bank robberies. We drove the teller insane twice depositing and withdrawing the same fifteen hundred dollars, but I figured they owed us for catching their robbers. At least I didn't have to worry about running into my parents, since I'd told them I'd be here.

After that, we had to walk down the street and annoy the teller at Curtis's bank so we could temporarily deposit the money into his account.

But at the end of an hour, Curtis, Victor, and I all had deposit slips showing totals of $1492.43 in our bank accounts—for the sake of realism, Curtis had insisted upon an odd, not exact, figure. And Lani and Haleigh had their money safely back in their own bank accounts.

★ ★ ★

That night over hamburger stroganoff, I showed my dad a bank deposit statement that read "$1492.43."

"Thatta boy!" he said. "There. Now doesn't that give you a nice feeling of satisfaction, seeing that little piece of paper?"

I couldn't deny it—mostly because it would mean the punishment to end all punishments if that little piece of paper hadn't been there.

The next day, we met the girls at the gravel pit again. I admit I was nervous. I could only imagine what their devilish little minds would put us up to.

"At the start of the summer, Lani's mom and my mom decided that we had to do volunteer work all summer long," Haleigh said. "Like we'd committed some crime, not just finished a grueling year of school."

We could relate.

"So they signed us up for something called Junior Community Service," Haleigh went on. "And we've gone every Saturday for six weeks. But we want this Saturday off."

"What are you saying?" Curtis said. "You want us to

185

do your volunteer work this week?"

Lani nodded. "This Saturday. At the Evergreen Assisted Living Center. You'll be doing makeovers on the women."

"Saint Embarrassus," Victor mumbled, able to speak around Lani at last.

Still, a deal was a deal. So that Saturday afternoon, we showed up at the Evergreen Assisted Living Center. The woman behind the front desk looked surprised to see us.

"*You're* the kids from Junior Community Service?" she said.

"Yeah," Curtis said. "So?"

"So I was just expecting . . ." She shook her head. "The women are waiting for you in the dayroom." She pointed us to a doorway down the hall.

The dayroom was surprisingly homey: a large sunroom with big picture windows and comfortable couches covered in plastic. A huge bouquet of hydrangeas sat on the wicker coffee table, along with all the beauty supplies.

There were eight women waiting for us, all at least

seventy. Each wore a robe or sweatsuit. Two were in wheelchairs, but there were also canes and walkers leaning up against the wall. The room smelled like a dozen different powders and lotions—not to mention a couple of unpleasant body odors.

But Curtis confronted the women with a huge grin on his face. He introduced us all, then said, "Someone told us you gals are interested in a little makeover. But I know that can't be right, because you all already look so pretty!"

Eight yellowed but beaming smiles greeted us.

"Oh, well," Curtis said. "Let's get that hair in curlers anyway! Let's get those fingernails painted!"

I admit there are times when Curtis's utter self-confidence and larger-than-life personality annoys me. But this was not one of those times.

That said, none of the three of us knew beans about makeovers. Fortunately, there's this thing about women and hair and makeup: They've done it so many times in their lives that you can give them a little push, like pick up an eyebrow pencil and wave it in their direction, and off they go.

As they worked, we talked.

"How long have you lived in Tacoma?" I asked Mrs. Duffy, a frail-looking woman with short hair parted like a man's.

"Oh, far too long!" she said. "Would have moved away years ago if my husband hadn't wanted to live near his mother. But the city's much better than it used to be. It was such an ugly, backward place."

"Now *that* is the danged-darn truth," said Mrs. Forsythe, who had a Southern accent. "What was *that* about?"

"Inferiority complex," said Mrs. Gladstein, a platinum blonde with saggy stockings. "It never got over being outdone by Seattle up north. But jealousy makes a city bitter and small-minded. Just like people. One of my brothers was a different person after my other brother bought that mansion out on American Lake."

"I like that Tacoma is a city of secrets," said Mrs. Martin, a plump woman in a flowered housecoat.

"Secrets?" I said, trying—unsuccessfully—to help Mrs. Duffy with her eyeliner. How were you supposed to use that stuff without poking a person in the eye?

Mrs. Martin preened in a hand mirror. "Oh, yes. People expect a big city like Seattle to have secrets. They

188

don't expect it in Tacoma. But what people forget is that Tacoma *was* a big city. That makes its secrets even more interesting, because most people have forgotten all about them. But we women? We don't forget."

I hadn't expected to be interested in anything these women had to say. Suddenly I was.

"What kind of secrets?" Victor asked.

"Well, if we *told* you," Mrs. Forsythe said coyly, "they wouldn't be secrets, would they?"

"We know one of the city's secrets," I found myself saying. "The China Tunnels. We've even been down in them." I wasn't sure what made me say this. It just seemed that since the women were sharing things, we should too.

Mrs. Duffy looked up at me from her wheelchair with a big smile. "Oh, you *have*, have you? So they really exist! I've been hearing about those tunnels my whole life. Any chance you'll show me where they are?"

Mrs. Duffy was probably ninety years old. So of course I said, "I'd be *happy* to take you down in those old tunnels! But it's cold down there, so you'll have to bring a sweater."

"*Ha!*" Mrs. Duffy said. "It's a *deal!*"

"I know a secret," said a woman who hadn't spoken before. "Something I haven't thought about in a long time." It was Mrs. Yee, a small Asian woman with nimble fingers.

"Oh?" Curtis said, clearly trying to humor her. "What secret is that?"

Mrs. Yee raised an eyebrow. "There's a treasure hidden right here in Tacoma."

"Is that right?" I said with a smile. But when I looked over at her face, I saw that her mouth was even, her jaw firm. Victor, Curtis, and I all met one another's eyes. The air in the room smelled better now, of perfumed face powder and fingernail polish.

"What kind of treasure?" Victor asked quietly.

"It all happened over a hundred years ago, in 1885. It was the year Tacoma kicked out the Chinese people."

"A *terrible* time," Mrs. Duffy said. "Just goes to show that Tacoma had its faults even before it lost its rivalry with Seattle."

"Back then, the Chinese were all anyone could talk about," Mrs. Yee went on. "Everything that was bad with the city was all their fault. They were treated like dogs, or worse. Finally, the city ordered all the Chinese to leave town by Tuesday, November third. One group of Chinese men decided to get back at the city. They'd leave town, sure, but only after robbing the city bank. They knew the combination to the vault because none of the white people noticed the old Chinese man who cleaned the bank floors while they worked. And they knew they could get in and out of the bank without detection because they'd helped dig the China Tunnels, and they knew about a secret entrance in the basement of the building."

The China Tunnels! We knew for a fact that they did exist. Did that mean that Mrs. Yee's story, whatever it was, might be true too?

"But a woman named Lei-Lei Tang was out tending her chrysanthemums," Mrs. Yee continued. "And she overheard the men planning to rob the bank. Lei-Lei hated the idea. Not only was it wrong to steal, Lei-Lei was certain the white people would blame the Chinese people left behind, and punish them harshly.

"That night, Monday night, the men went through with the plan to rob the bank, stealing more than twenty thousand dollars. But Lei-Lei was watching. Then she made a decision of her own. While the men were preparing to leave town, she decided to steal the money from them and sneak it back into the bank vault. That way, the Chinese men would accuse one another of taking the money, and the white people in town would never know about the bank robbery in the first place.

"Lei-Lei took the money, intending to return it to the bank. But one of the men quickly noticed that the money was gone. They began searching Chinatown and the China Tunnels for the missing loot. Rather than draw suspicion to herself and knowing she'd never get back into the vault that night, Lei-Lei hid the money in a safe place, planning to return it to the bank early the next morning while everyone else was still asleep.

"But something terrible happened early the next morning. Before she could return the money, white men came to Chinatown. Lei-Lei tried to slip away to get the money from its hiding place, but they wouldn't let her. And that Tuesday morning happened to be the day that the whole Chinese community was rounded up by the city of Tacoma and put on a train to Portland."

"Did Lei-Lei ever come back to Tacoma to get the money?" Curtis asked.

Mrs. Yee shook her head. "For months, she tried to come back to return the money to the bank, but she couldn't afford to make the trip."

"*Why?*" Mrs. Forsythe said. "After what Tacoma had done to her, why'd she want to return it at all? It sounds like the city got exactly what it deserved!"

Mrs. Forsythe had a point. Still, I knew why Lei-Lei had tried so hard to come back. It was the reason Curtis, Victor, and I had broken into Mrs. Shelby's house: to make it clear that we didn't steal, that we were better than she was. Lei-Lei wanted to prove, once and for all, that she was better than the people who had done her own people so wrong.

"A few months after the incident, Lei-Lei stopped trying to come back," Mrs. Yee went on. "She had learned something that changed her mind. Eventually, she died in Portland, in a home surrounded by a big garden of chrysanthemums. But before she died, she told her daughter the whole story. Who told her daughter. Who told me."

"Lei-Lei was your great-grandmother?" Mrs. Martin said, but I wasn't surprised. I had already figured that part out, and I knew that Curtis and Victor had too.

Mrs. Yee nodded.

"Did she ever tell you where the money was?" Curtis asked.

"No," Mrs. Yee said. "Lei-Lei never told anyone that. I guess she decided that the obligation to return the money ended with her. She didn't want the money either, since it wasn't hers to begin with. But my mother did say that her mother told her it was in a very safe place where no one would ever find it."

As Mrs. Yee finished her story, the room fell so quiet you could almost hear the fingernail polish drying. I had no way of knowing if the story was true, but I was certain that Mrs. Yee *thought* it was. Was there really something to the idea that women were the keepers of secrets in a community? After all, back in Lei-Lei's day, the Chinese men had secrets from the white people, but the Chinese women knew the secrets of the men, and also had secrets of their own.

I also thought how ironic it was that if my dad hadn't wanted to see my bank balance, we wouldn't have had to make that deal with Haleigh and Lani, and we wouldn't have ever heard this story.

"I hate to say it," Curtis said quietly, "but we're just about done here."

I looked around the room. Curtis was right. The women had been curled and powdered and rouged and lipsticked beyond recognition. Technically, they looked ridiculous; none of them were exactly cover-girl material to begin with, and while they'd applied their own makeup countless times before, these were women with shaking fingers and terrible eyesight. Meanwhile, Curtis, Victor, and I had been absolutely no help whatsoever—and had probably made things worse.

But the afternoon hadn't been about the quality of our makeup and hairstyling. It was about the expressions on the faces of these old ladies, which were shining like seven-year-olds at the gates to Disneyland.

"Oh," Mrs. Gladstein said sadly.

"Yes," said Mrs. Duffy, tears forming in her eyes. "Well, thank you all for coming to visit with us."

"Thank *you*," Curtis said. "And do you mind if we come back sometime to visit?"

"We'd *love* that," Mrs. Martin said.

For once, Curtis wasn't lying. I knew we would go back to visit these women. Before then, maybe I could figure out how in the world you're supposed to use eyeliner without poking the person in the eye.

WEEK 8:

Sunk

Do I really need to say that we spent the rest of the weekend trying to figure out where Lei-Lei might have hidden that money?

"Mrs. Yee's mother told her it was in a very safe place," Curtis said for the hundredth time. "That means that, wherever Lei-Lei hid it, it's probably still there."

"But Mrs. Yee also said that her mother told her it was someplace where no one would ever find it," Victor reminded him.

It was Sunday afternoon, and the three of us were pacing back and forth inside the bomb shelter. We had

only three weeks left to complete Project Sweet Life—
to somehow make the entire seven thousand dollars
we needed to prove to our dads that we had spent the
summer working. The Lei-Lei Tang fortune—more than
twenty thousand dollars in 1885 money—would be more
than enough. But if we didn't find it, Curtis, Victor, and
I might never get to see one another again, except in
school.

Victor stopped pacing. "It's pointless!" he said. "We'll
never find it."

"It's *not* pointless," Curtis said, determined to keep
pacing. "We *will!*"

"It *is* pointless," I said, unsure whether to pace or not.
"But we still can't give up. There's too much at stake."

We were alternating between hope (Curtis) and
despair (Victor) and everything in between (me). It didn't
help that it was the second week in August, and after a
cool, comfortable summer, a heat wave had descended
on the city like an itchy wool blanket. It should have
been cool inside an underground concrete pillbox, but
it wasn't, especially since we'd sold our air-conditioner
seven weeks earlier. It felt like we were in one of those
metal boxes you see in prison movies, where they put

prisoners out in the yard to bake in the sun.

As he was pacing, Curtis happened to pass *Trains and Totem Poles*, the book on the history of Tacoma.

"Wait," he said. "Maybe there's a clue in here."

I took this to be a very bad sign. If Curtis was resorting to actual research, he was clearly at the end of his rope.

But he opened the book and started reading the section about the city's expulsion of the Chinese.

"Well," Curtis said, "everything Mrs. Yee said was true. The city kicked out all the Chinese on November third, 1885—a Tuesday, just like she said."

"That's interesting," I said. "But even if the story is true, Lei-Lei could have hidden that money anywhere. We still don't have any idea where to look."

"Not anywhere," Victor said thoughtfully. "It would have to be somewhere *in* the China Tunnels."

"Which we and lots of others have already explored and didn't find anything," I said.

"Or in some area around Chinatown," Victor said.

"Which doesn't even exist anymore!" I said. We'd already gone over this again and again.

"No, wait," Victor said. "Let's just think about this logically. Years after Chinatown had been destroyed,

Lei-Lei was still telling her daughter that the money was in a very safe place and that no one would ever find it. So what are the possibilities?"

"She could have buried it," Curtis said.

"I doubt it," Victor said. "It was supposed to be a temporary hiding place, remember?"

"Then where?" I said. "What's left?"

Victor pursed his lips. *"Think.* Where could Lei-Lei have hidden the money? Where *would* she have hidden the money?"

"I don't know!" I said, exasperated.

But suddenly Victor's eyes grew wide. "I do."

"You do?" I said. "Tell me more."

"What do we know?" Victor said, suddenly excited. "The money was stolen from the men and hidden by Lei-Lei late Monday night. The whole Chinese community, including Lei-Lei, was rounded up and kicked out of town early Tuesday morning. And on Wednesday, the whole Chinese settlement was burned down, then pushed into the waters of Commencement Bay. But when Lei-Lei hid the money on Monday night, she didn't mean for it to be hidden forever. What kind of temporary hiding place is *that* good?"

"I don't know," Curtis said. "What kind?"

"Don't you see?" Victor said. "Something happened after she hid it on Monday night that changed everything."

"Yeah," Curtis said. "She got shipped off to Oregon!"

Victor shook his head hard. "No! Don't you see? The answer is so *obvious*."

It was late in the summer, and I was now *very* tired of cryptic talk and dramatic pauses. "Victor," I said, "get to the point. Where do you think the money's hidden?"

"In the water offshore from where Chinatown used to be!" he said. "Maybe Lei-Lei hid the money underneath a dock, or just under the tide line. It was only supposed to be for a few hours. But then the white men pushed the whole settlement into the bay, right on top of the money."

Curtis and I thought about this. Was Victor jumping to conclusions now? Maybe so, but it was still a pretty good theory.

"Mrs. Yee did say that in the months after the Chinese got kicked out, Lei-Lei tried to come back to Tacoma to get the money," Curtis said. "But then she gave up. She must have finally learned that Chinatown had been burned and pushed into the bay. That's how she would know that the money was somewhere where no one would ever find it." Curtis looked at me, blue eyes blazing. "I think Victor is right. Big-time bonus points!"

"But if it really is under all those burned-up shacks and shanties," I said, "how do *we* get to it?"

"It *was* under them," Victor said. "That doesn't mean it's *still* under them. It's been over a century since this happened. All the wood from the shanties would have long since rotted away in the water."

"Well, how do we know that whatever the money was stored in hasn't rotted away too?" I said. "If it was a metal or wooden box or a leather satchel, that'd be long gone."

"But Mrs. Yee said the money *is* safely hidden," Victor pointed out. "If that's what her great-grandmother told her grandmother, it must have been stored in something waterproof, like porcelain. The Chinese were big on porcelain. There's a reason why china is called 'china,' you know."

"Sunken treasure?" I said, finally giving in to the wild speculation. "This is the coolest thing we've done so far!"

"Well, what are we waiting for?" Curtis said. "Let's go get ourselves some scuba equipment!"

"Not so fast," Victor said. "Before we do anything else, I still need to check some things out at the library."

"The library again?" Curtis said, clearly disappointed. But this made me feel better, because it meant he was back to his usual research-hating self.

Down at the main branch of the Tacoma Public Library, we didn't even bother asking the research librarian for help.

After a half hour or so, Victor emerged from the online newspaper archives with a satisfied grin on his face.

"It's all true," he whispered. "There really was a bank robbery at Tacoma's biggest bank, the National Bank of Commerce, the night of Monday, November second, 1885. Over twenty thousand dollars was taken. Can you imagine what that would be worth today?"

"No," Curtis said. "What would it be worth?"

Victor gestured back to the stacks. "I could go look it up."

"What do you think it is?" I said. "Gold?"

"Well, I don't think bank notes were in widespread use yet," Victor said. "So yeah, it's probably gold or silver. I could go look that up, too."

Curtis recoiled like a vampire from daylight. "Let's just get out of this place!"

But as long as we were downtown, we decided to stop in at the Paper Lantern, the Chinese restaurant where we'd learned about the entrance to the China Tunnels.

We took a booth, and the same older woman who had served us before came to give us menus.

"We found what was right in front of the faces," Curtis told her, referring to the clue she'd given us in the fortune cookie. The woman seemed much more relaxed than she had before. Maybe it was because she was alone this time; I didn't see her husband back in the kitchen.

"Did you now?" the woman said.

"But it didn't lead where we thought it would," Curtis went on. "So now we're looking for something else. Something that was hidden a long time ago by a woman named Lei-Lei Tang."

Her face registered absolutely nothing.

"You know who she is!" I said. I was sure I was right. When you mention a name to someone, they usually react in one of two ways: recognition or confusion. They never look completely blank.

The woman flattened a menu. "I suppose I've heard that name before."

"Is it true?" Curtis asked. "Does the money really exist?"

"Who can say?" she said.

"We think we know where it is," I said. I think we all knew that if there was anyone we could trust, it was this woman.

"That money has been missing for far too long," the woman said. I realized we didn't even know her name.

Victor fiddled with the soy sauce. "If we find it, we won't keep it," he said. "Not all of it, anyway. Just seven thousand dollars that we need for . . . something. The rest . . ." He looked over at the jar on the counter, the one for donations for the monument to commemorate the expulsion of the Chinese. "The rest we'll donate to the Reconciliation Project."

Even as Curtis was saying this, I knew it was exactly the right thing to do.

"In that case," she said with a smile, "I hope you do find it. Now why don't I make you some lunch?"

"Um," Victor said. "We don't have any money."

She winked at us. "That's okay. This one's on me."

It may have been the best meal I've ever eaten. The vegetables were fresh and crunchy, and the meat was light and juicy. It wasn't too salty or too sweet. I like my mom's cooking, but this was better.

After lunch, she gave us each a fortune cookie that we broke open on the sidewalk outside the restaurant. This time she hadn't made any additions to the fortunes, so we were getting the unfiltered truth.

I read my fortune. *"Mind the smallest detail,"* I said, *"or you may have to begin again."*

"A familiar face is proof that you're not long lost," Curtis read.

"A seat for the weary is always welcome," Victor said. He sighed. "Fortune cookies. They're so vague, they can be applied to any situation."

"Now what?" I asked.

"What else?" Curtis said. "Now we do some diving!"

The good news is that Curtis, Victor, and I were licensed scuba divers. Better still, in our state fifteen was the age that we could legally do a dive on our own.

The bad news is that none of us had our own equipment. And renting masks and fins and tanks and regulators and weight-belts is expensive.

Did I mention we had no money?

We looked up the nearest dive shop, then rode our bikes over there. It was part of an old marina in Point Defiance Park, way north of downtown.

The Rocky Bottom was a little shack of a store hidden in a maze of creaky docks and warped wooden boathouses. Curtis stepped up to the man behind the counter. He was brawny and sunwashed, with one green eye and one blue. He looked exactly like a diver should look; there was even a tattoo of Ariel from *The Little Mermaid* on his shoulder.

"We need some diving equipment for a couple of days," Curtis said bluntly. "But we don't have any money."

"Well," said the man, "that's definitely a problem."

"Just hear us out," Curtis said. "We know for a fact where a huge treasure is located in Puget Sound. It cannot miss. If you let us have the equipment for free, we'll give you five percent of the total take of anything we find."

The man thought for a second. "That is an interesting proposal. How about this instead? You three work for me for one full day, and I'll lend you the equipment you need for up to three days."

Curtis, Victor, and I eyed one another. It wasn't the worst bargain in the world.

"Okay," Curtis said earnestly. "But you're really going to regret it when we find that treasure."

"This time next week, I know I'll be absolutely kicking myself," the dive-shop guy said. "See you tomorrow morning."

It's a long ride from our houses to Point Defiance, so we had to leave early in order to be there by a reasonable hour. It was the earliest I'd gotten up since summer began. In spite of the risk of the total failure of Project Sweet Life, I still considered the fact that I'd been able to sleep in every day since the Saturday of our garage sale to be something of an achievement.

"You boys know how to clean a boat?" said Bill, the dive-shop guy.

"My dad has a boat," Curtis said. This was true.

We'd been out on it lots of times. But even I knew that cleaning a boat, especially one that's been in salt water, was a chore and a half. I'd heard Curtis complain about it often enough.

Bill led us down to the docks, then winched a sailboat out of the water and up into one of the barnlike boathouses where vessels were dry-docked. Seagulls rustled up in the rafters. The August heat had caused some sort of algae bloom out in Puget Sound, so the whole area smelled like rotting seaweed.

"The boat's been moored all summer and most of the spring," he said.

"In salt water?" Curtis said. "*That* was stupid! Who's the idiotic owner, anyway?"

"I am," Bill said.

"Ah!" Curtis said. "And I bet you had an *excellent* reason for keeping it moored, don't you?"

"It's a rental," Bill said. "Which means I want it right back in the water when you're done. But nice save." He turned toward the exit. "Between the three of you, you should be able to clean it inside and out before the end of the day."

* * *

The day had started out hot and grew hotter with each passing hour. And that stuffy, stinky boathouse wasn't air-conditioned.

We started with the hull. It was covered with scum and something rough and bumpy.

"*Barnacles?*" I said. "There are actual *barnacles* growing on this thing."

"That's one of the problems with salt water," Curtis said.

We got to scraping.

"Wait," I said as we worked. "If Lei-Lei's money is hidden in a porcelain pot, how are we ever going to find it? Won't it be completely buried under barnacles and mussels by now? It's been over a hundred years."

"Not if it really is stored in porcelain," Victor explained. "Barnacles don't grow on glass or porcelain. The glaze is too smooth. There's nothing for sea life to cling to. Fiberglass is completely different. It's basically the perfect surface for barnacles. But it's light and it's cheap, which is why they make boats out of it."

In terms of scum, the only thing worse than the fiberglass hull was the name of the boat, *The Ruby*

Slipper, spelled out in pewter.

"Oh, pewter's the *worst*," Curtis said. "But at least it doesn't rust."

It was well into the afternoon before we were finally done with the hull. Then we flushed and cleaned the engine and turned to the boat's interior. Right away, we discovered water sloshing around in the bilge, which is the space between the floor and the bottom of the boat.

"It's no big deal," Curtis said. "We just have to open the drain plug down in the bilge. Someone get me a wrench."

So we got a wrench and opened up the drain plug, a small hole in the lowest part of the boat. Foul water spilled onto the wooden slats of the boathouse floor. Then we hosed the whole thing down.

Next we cleaned the seats and dashboard and paneling where salt water had splashed and evaporated. For the record, salt water had splashed *everywhere*, along with something dried and sticky.

I wrinkled my nose. "Dried beer," I said.

"It's a rental," Curtis said.

Finally, we finished. We pushed the boat toward the docks, then winched it back down into the water.

We went inside to get Bill. He was, I swear, actually

sharpening a fishing spear. How fitting was that?

"We're done," Curtis said. "Is it okay if we get fitted for our equipment now? That way we can get an early start tomorrow morning."

"Sure thing," Bill said. "But let's go take a look at your work first, okay?"

We followed Bill outside. He strolled calmly toward the docks. But then he slammed to a stop, his whole body snapping to attention.

"What is it?" I said, but even as I said it, I saw: *The Ruby Slipper* was sinking.

"How—?" Victor started.

"Please tell me you replaced the drain plug!" Bill said.

Curtis immediately reddened. "Uh oh."

Bill suddenly broke into laughter. Relief swept through me: We'd screwed up, but not so badly that he couldn't laugh about it.

Bill kept laughing, and it was pretty clear he was laughing at us.

"Uh," I said, "don't we have to get the boat out before it sinks?"

Bill wiped tears from his eyes. "Hey, it's a small hole. We've got a few minutes before it sinks completely."

Sure enough, a few minutes later, we had the boat winched up onto the dock again. But a lot of water had gotten inside the body—salt water choked with algae and little pieces of loose seaweed that were already drying in the intense heat.

Bill faced us. "So," he said, "I'll see you guys again same time tomorrow morning, right?"

Curtis sighed. "Yeah. You will."

As we were walking back to our bikes, I dug my hands in my pockets. I felt something in there and pulled out a little strip of paper—my fortune from our lunch at the Paper Lantern.

I read it to myself. Then I started to laugh.

"What's so funny?" Victor said.

I read out loud, *"Mind the smallest detail, or you may have to begin again."*

The next day, we rode our bikes back to the dive shop. It was blistering outside, even hotter than the day before. The inside of that boathouse felt like a crematorium left on all night.

Cleaning that crusty seaweed was a challenge, but at least we didn't have to scrub the hull again. When we were done, we made absolutely sure that the drain plug was tightly sealed.

We went back inside the dive shop to get Bill.

"Okay," Curtis said. "This time, we're really, really done."

Bill checked to make sure that the boat hadn't sunk again and was satisfied at last.

"Okay, let's get you three fitted," he said. "With weather like this, I'll bet you can't wait to get into that water. I'll just need a major credit card for the deposit."

Neither Curtis, Victor, nor I spoke. What could we say? None of us had credit cards. We were fifteen years old!

"Excuse me?" Curtis said at last.

"The deposit?" Bill said. "I won't actually charge anything, not if you bring the equipment back. It's just in case you run off with our stuff."

Bill stared at us.

We stared at him.

Finally, a smile cracked his face. *"Kidding!"* he said. "Leave your student I.D. cards, and we'll call it a deal."

It was already too late in the day to try to get in a dive, so the next day, Thursday, we rode our bikes back to the dive shop to pick up the equipment, then rode all the way downtown. How did we manage to carry our tanks and the rest of the gear on our bikes?

Don't ask. I don't want to relive it.

But eventually we made it.

Back in the nineteenth century, Tacoma's Chinatown had been located on the stretch of coastline just north of the city center, a narrow strip of land at the base of the greenbelt where the exit to the China Tunnels had emerged from the ivy. Now the greenbelt was cut off from the beach by a busy concrete parkway and a set of train tracks. Thea Foss Park, a forgotten little stretch of grass, juts up from tideflats to the south, so that's where we went to lock our bikes and sort out our equipment.

Looking north from that park, there's no sign of Chinatown now, not even a monument. In fact, the only signs of life are the rotting pilings of some abandoned piers and a concrete granary farther down the beach. Because it's industrial, the whole area was deserted, despite being just a few hundred yards from the city center.

"So this is it," I said. The water itself was dark, almost crude-oil black.

"This is the least appealing dive site I've ever seen," Victor said.

"All the more reason why we should get it over with," Curtis said, slipping into the water.

On the plus side, it felt good. The water of Puget Sound never gets much above fifty degrees, so it was the perfect antidote to the blistering heat.

On the negative side, there was a steep drop-off only a few yards from the beach. And the water was murky.

Really murky.

Puget Sound is always murky, but the weird August algae bloom had made it worse. And it wasn't just algae: the Puyallup River, which emptied into Commencement Bay right behind us, muddied the water with silt from the mountain glaciers. Visibility was a few feet at best. It was like you could feel the sediment clinging to you, coating you with slime, weighing you down.

Since there were three of us, we couldn't split up into dive buddies, so we stayed with one another at all times. This was especially important given the low visibility.

Under the water, we stopped at the edge of the sharp drop-off—a steep slope just off from the beach that quickly disappeared into the gloom. The whole area above and below the drop-off was covered with trash, mostly bottles and scraps of white plastic. I'd never understood why people needed to use the ocean as their personal garbage dump.

Curtis reached out, picked up one of the discarded bottles, and showed it to Victor and me.

It looked odd somehow. Not like a pop bottle, that's for sure. I tried to make out the words written on the side, but they looked odd too—not like English.

I squinted through the fog of my mask and through the murk of that water. They weren't words at all but little squiggles, almost like Chinese writing.

It took me a second to realize what this meant.

This glass bottle was something from the Chinese settlement!

I looked more closely at the garbage strewn around us.

It wasn't discarded plastic I was seeing, but porcelain: plates and saucers, their blue or rose-latticed borders still visible. Little teacups. Pots and tureens and long-necked vases.

Victor had been right when he'd said that barnacles

didn't grow on porcelain or glass. He'd also been right about the fact that all the wood from the settlement itself had long since rotted away.

Most of the porcelain was in pieces. This made sense. Since the whole settlement had been burned and pushed into the water, it stood to reason that a lot of it would have cracked and shattered. But did that mean that whatever the money was in had been broken too?

We rooted through the pieces of porcelain and glass—all that remained of what had once been a whole community. We groped our way back and forth along the upper shelf, before the bottom dropped off into darkness. To the south and north of the dive site, parallel to the beach, the glass and porcelain remnants eventually petered out. We had isolated exactly where the settlement must have been.

We brought the intact pots to the surface to open them up, but we didn't find anything with twenty thousand dollars in gold or silver inside.

We had no choice but to go deeper, down the steep drop-off. So down we went, crawling along the muddy bottom.

We found more glass and porcelain, but had no better

luck than we'd had at the shallower level. And the deeper you dive, the higher the pressure is, and the more quickly you use up your oxygen. So by the time we reached sixty feet, we were burning through our air pretty fast. Eventually we had no choice but to surface.

"Nothing," Victor said. "Not a thing." Truthfully, without his glasses, Victor was kind of worthless for searching underwater. But he was right that none of us had found anything.

The water sloshed around us, smelling of brine and seaweed. There was a rainbow sheen of spilled gasoline roiling on the surface—runoff from the industrial tideflats.

"We need to go deeper," Curtis said. "We have to come back tomorrow."

The tide was out, and I'd found a flat rock to sit on. "That doesn't make any sense," I said. "If Lei-Lei only hid the money for a day, she wouldn't have hid it that deep. She *couldn't* have."

"Maybe it slid," Curtis said. "But it's gotta be here somewhere."

"No, it doesn't," Victor said. "Maybe someone else found it. We can't be the first people ever to have dived here." He had a point. Lots of people had probably dived here, looking for salvage. Why hadn't this occurred to us before?

"Or maybe it broke open and the gold sank into the mud," Victor went on. "Or maybe it was never here to begin with. All I know is I can't bear the thought of bringing this equipment all the way back to the dive shop to get more air, then carrying it all the way back here tomorrow."

"We *have* to," Curtis said. "There's only two weeks of summer left. If we don't get that seven thousand dollars soon, we're sunk!"

Barnacles poked me in the rear, making me squirm. I didn't say anything. Victor didn't either. What could we say? Curtis had made a good point, too.

Victor sighed, slumping in the mud. But then he jerked upright again. Like me, he'd sat on something sharp.

"What is it?" I said.

He reached down into the water and pulled out an oddly familiar object.

It was a ceramic statue of Mr. Moneybags, his arms outstretched. He had the cane in one hand, but it was partly broken off.

"Where'd *that* come from?" I said.

It wasn't our statue, of course. That was safely back at the bomb shelter. For one thing, this one was covered with mud, like it had been underwater for a while. But— what a coincidence!—it looked exactly like ours.

"It's a sign," Curtis said suddenly. "Don't you see? A familiar face!"

"What?" Victor said.

"Remember my fortune cookie? *A familiar face is proof that you're not long lost.* Well, this is the familiar face!"

Victor and I looked at each other. He had been right when he'd said those fortune cookies had been pretty vague. But twice now, they had applied directly to the situation at hand. It was incredible.

"Look," Curtis said. "I know it's just a fortune cookie. But the fact that this was right here all afternoon and we never spotted it because of the murk or whatever, well, that means there might be something *else* that's right here and we didn't spot it, either."

I had to admit this made sense, enough to make me feel at least a little optimistic again.

★ ★ ★

The next day, Friday, we rode back to the dive shop one more time to pick up our refilled air tanks.

"Buck up," Bill said. "You think Pizarro found the golden city of El Dorado in a day? Or Ponce de León and the Fountain of Youth?"

"Pizarro *never* found the golden city of El Dorado," Victor said. "And Ponce de León didn't find the Fountain of Youth either."

Bill grinned. "Oops. My bad."

I could tell the mood was grim when Curtis didn't say anything back.

By the time we'd ridden the scuba equipment back to the dive site, I was already exhausted. My skin itched; even though I'd been wearing sunblock the day before, I finally had the sunburn my parents had been warning me about all summer—not to mention some weird rash breaking out on my legs, either from the algae bloom or some toxic chemical wafting over from the tideflats. This was turning out to be the most difficult Project Sweet Life scheme by far. I could only hope it would be worth it.

But despite the fact that we went back over all the ground we'd examined and then went even deeper than before—ninety feet at least—we saw nothing that might be used to store money.

Before we knew it, our tanks were out of air.

We sat in the shallow water of that pathetic little beach for a long time. The wake from passing boats lapped at our armpits and jogged our empty tanks. It was no longer the cool temperature that kept me slumped on my little rocky shelf of a seat. It was that I knew exactly what leaving meant: We were one step closer to the end of our friendship.

Curtis and Victor didn't move either. They knew what I knew.

But we couldn't stay in that water forever. As the sun sank lower in the sky, we all stood and slowly slopped our way to shore.

I stopped suddenly, water dripping down my body. "Wait," I said.

Victor turned. "What?"

"The last fortune cookie," I said, just above a whisper.

"What about it?" Curtis said.

"What was it?" I said, looking at Victor. "What was your fortune?"

He thought for a second. "Something about a place to sit when you're tired."

"*A seat for the weary is always welcome,*" Curtis recited. He stared at me. "Dave? What is it? What are you thinking?"

I turned back to the water. "It's crazy. I know it is! I mean, what are the odds? But I'd never forgive myself if I didn't check."

"What?" Curtis said. "Check *what*?"

"*A seat for the weary is always welcome!*" I said. "That rock I was sitting on—it was flat, almost like a seat."

I fumbled in the water, looking for the shelf-like rock.

"Help me!" I said. "Help me get this to the surface!"

I saw right away that it wasn't a rock. It was a rectangular box covered with barnacles and mussels.

"It's not porcelain," Curtis said.

"That was our mistake!" I said. "Assuming it was porcelain!"

We carried it to the beach.

"It's heavy," Curtis said. He didn't say it, but I knew we were all thinking the same thing: *like it's filled with gold!*

I grabbed a rock and started scraping at the surface.

"Metal," Curtis said. "It's made of metal!"

"Not just metal," Victor said excitedly. "Pewter. Which doesn't rust!"

We kept scraping at the box until we could make out its general shape.

"Saint Barnaclees!" Victor said. "It's a tea caddy!"

"What?" I said.

"Something the Chinese stored tea in. They used to be bigger than they are now, because the Chinese drank a lot of tea. And it would be airtight, to keep the tea fresh."

At that moment, I scraped away enough of the barnacles on the top to see the engraving there. It was a flower.

No, not just a flower.

A chrysanthemum! Lei-Lei's favorite flower!

"Open it," Curtis said. "Open it!"

I turned to Victor. "You do it," I said. "This was your idea."

So he did. He had to pry it with his weight-belt buckle.

We all held our breath.

Finally, he forced the lid open.

We all leaned forward so fast, our heads almost clunked together.

It was dark inside the container. Dark and wet.

Victor reached inside the caddy. His forehead furrowed. Then he probed deeper still, fumbling around with his hand.

"Well?" Curtis said. "*Well?*"

Victor lifted his hand out of the container and opened his palm.

Thick brown sludge dripped down from his fingers. It splattered against the water. For a second, I thought I saw little numbers—vague ones and twos and fives and zeros—floating on the surface of the water, like the sheen of gasoline we'd seen earlier. They looked like ink that had been lifted off paper. And almost immediately, they dissolved away.

"What's that?" Curtis said, meaning the sludge.

"All there is inside," Victor said.

"Wait," Curtis said. "What are you saying?"

"I'm saying," Victor said, "that I think I was wrong about Lei-Lei's money not being in bank notes. And at some point over the last century, the container leaked."

WEEK 9:

The Very Last Chance

"Project Sweet Life?" I said. "*Ha!* That's a laugh! It sure hasn't made our life very sweet."

It was Tuesday afternoon in the third week of August, the week after we'd learned that if we had found Lei-Lei's money, it had long since turned to Cream of Wheat. The heat wave still hadn't let up, and we could barely stand being in the bomb shelter, even with the door propped open.

"And summer's almost over!" I went on. "Even if we get seven thousand dollars tomorrow, that only gives us one week off before school. Some sweet life!

227

We've worked our butts off all summer long—and for nothing!"

Part of me was mad at Curtis. After all, Project Sweet Life had been his idea in the first place. But I couldn't stay angry. We'd all signed on knowing the risks. It wasn't Curtis's fault that we'd failed. Who knew it would end up being so hard to make a simple seven thousand dollars?

"We didn't fail," Victor said, as if reading my mind. "We found Lei-Lei's money, and we guessed almost the right number of jelly beans. We even caught the bank robber. We've just had a run of bad luck."

"But we didn't get the money," Curtis said. "Who cares if we were right about those things? We didn't get the money! So yeah, we did fail. Now we're going to pay the price."

I thought, *Wow, even Curtis has given up!*

"It matters," Victor said. "If it hadn't been for Lani and Haleigh, we would've won that ten thousand dollars. If it hadn't been for Mrs. Shelby, we would've caught the bank robbers."

Curtis just snorted in disgust. I'd never seen him so down.

"Wait," Victor said suddenly.

"What?" I said.

"The guy who broke into Mrs. Shelby's at the same time we did? He was one of the bank robbers, too, wasn't he?"

"Eddy?" I said. "Yeah, I guess."

"Well, what if we caught *him*? Wouldn't we get another hundred-thousand-dollar reward?"

I shrugged. "Maybe. What difference does it make? We don't know where he is."

Victor's eyes narrowed. "Maybe we do."

Curtis looked up.

"Remember when we were staking out Mrs. Shelby's house?" Victor said. "And remember how Eddy was also staking out her house at exactly the same time by pretending to be a plumber? Well, I just remembered something about his plumber's van. It had a Zone One parking sticker on his back bumper."

"That's right," I said. "I remember that, too."

"So to find Eddy, all we need to do is find his van. And if he had a Zone One parking sticker, we know where he parks."

"Is that enough to go on?" I said.

"Absolutely!" Curtis said suddenly. "It's just a *zone*. How big can a zone be? Piece-o-cake!"

Project Sweet Life was back in business. Meanwhile, the conclusion-jumping Curtis I knew was back too. All was right in the world.

That night after dinner, my mom presented my dad and me with one of her famous Tootsie Roll pies.

"What's this?" my dad said.

"It's a reward," she said. "For Dave."

"Me?" I said. "What'd I do?"

My mom smiled. "Well, mostly it's for what you didn't do. You've worked all summer long, and you haven't complained once, not since that first night when your dad said you had to get a job."

"That's true," my dad said, nodding. "Thatta boy."

Great, I thought. *For dessert tonight, we'll be offering a fine selection of guilt.*

"And you haven't left your wet towels lying in the bathroom," my mom went on, "and you never once ran late and had to ask us for a ride to the pool."

Okay, okay! I thought. This made me feel guilty *and*

stupid. Here I'd been thinking that the one thing we did succeed at this summer was outwitting our parents, but I hadn't even done *that* well. I'd just been lucky that my parents were so trusting.

"It wasn't any big deal," I said quietly.

"It was!" my mom said. "And I know exactly how you're going to want to spend some of that money you've been earning this summer."

"You do?" I said.

She nodded. "Back-to-school shopping!"

I didn't say what I was thinking, which was, *Wait. First, you unfairly force me to get a summer job a whole year before I'm supposed to. And now, despite the fact that you've paid for my back-to-school shopping every year until now, you also want me to spend the money I supposedly made on that job on back-to-school clothes? How is that fair?*

"I'm taking you to the mall this Saturday," my mom said. "I'll even spring for lunch!"

"Oh, you don't have to do that," I said.

"But I *want* to," my mom said.

"No, really," I said. "I'll do my back-to-school shopping Labor Day weekend."

231

"Dave, that's crazy. The mall will be mobbed."

"But Mom—"

My dad glanced over at me, eyes suddenly narrowing. I think his "surveyor's sense" was tingling something fierce.

So I had no choice but to nod at my mom and say, "Okay. Saturday it is."

But that's when I realized something pathetic: Despite what I'd said to Curtis and Victor, Project Sweet Life had stopped being about "the sweet life" a long time ago; now it was just about not getting caught. Every day meant another in a long string of lies. We could barely even go outside without worrying about being spotted by some random family member. But we couldn't stop now; we couldn't back out because the punishment would be unbearable.

This Saturday it would all come to an end, anyway. My mom would learn I had no money—unless we could somehow find Eddy and implicate him in the Capitol American bank robberies. Catching him was our very last chance. But even if we did catch him I still wouldn't have enough money to go shopping with my mom. It had taken Mrs. Shelby *weeks* to get the actual check.

Who knows? Maybe if we caught the bank robber, Capitol American would give me a loan.

We learned online that parking Zone 1 was, naturally enough, downtown. So the next day, Wednesday, we rode our bikes back there.

We saw right away that most of the street parking in the city center proper was one-hour-only, whether or not you had a parking sticker. It was just on the streets to the north and east of downtown, which were mostly apartment and condo buildings, that the Zone 1 parking stickers were valid.

"Now what?" I asked. "We just wander around Zone One until we see a white plumber's van?"

"I bet the plumber part was just one of those magnets you buy online to disguise a car," Curtis said. "I bet it peeled right off, so now it's just a plain white van."

"So that'll be even harder to find," I said.

"We could go back to the Paper Lantern and get some more fortunes," Curtis said. "I bet they'd tell us where to go!"

"Something tells me that won't work again," I said. "Why don't we let that be our backup plan?"

We zigzagged from one end of Zone 1, which butted up against Zone 2, to the other end, which ran into Zone 3.

It was hotter than ever outside—surface-of-the-planet-Venus hot. The sun glared down at us like a disapproving principal, giving me a headache. The heat rose up at us from the streets in great, suffocating waves. If you cooked an egg on the pavement, it would have fried as hard as an Egg McMuffin in a matter of seconds.

But we didn't see any white vans, plumber sticker or not.

"Maybe Eddy has a day job," I said, collapsing in the shade of a tree. It was only three in the afternoon, but staggering around in the Saharan heat had taken a lot out of us.

"He doesn't have a day job!" Curtis said. "He's a *thief*. Not having to work is the whole *point*."

"He still might have been out," Victor said.

So we went back the way we had come.

This time, we did find a white van, parked on one of

the side streets (and too close to a fire hydrant). It must have been parked there in just the last hour or so, because we'd passed this way before and hadn't seen it. Problem is, it didn't have a Zone 1 parking sticker.

"That's not it," I said. "Unless Eddy removed his sticker. But he's still parking in Zone One, so why in the world would he do that?"

A few blocks later, we spotted another white van. This one we might not have seen before, because it was parked in an alley between two buildings. We walked closer and saw that it had a Zone 1 parking sticker.

"Now what?" I said.

"Now we wait," Victor said.

We settled down in the meager shade of a spindly, dehydrated rhododendron and waited.

"We do have one advantage," Curtis said. "Eddy doesn't know we exist. He left the coffee shop before the waitress realized what we were up to—and given that he's guilty of the same crime she is, something tells me he's never visited her in jail. So I'm sure he thinks it was Mrs. Shelby, not us, who busted their operation. And I'm sure he has no idea we were in her house the day he broke in."

"Yeah," Victor said. "But there aren't that many teenagers downtown, remember?"

"What's your point?" I said.

"My point," Victor said, "is that we should still make sure Eddy doesn't see us."

We waited under that rhododendron for hours. We couldn't afford bottled water, so we took turns ducking into a nearby office building to use the drinking fountain. But none of us got restless. In fact, we were weirdly animated, excited that finding Eddy had proved to be so easy.

Then, finally, a skinny man in a paint-speckled jumpsuit emerged from the rear of a nearby building. He carried a spattered tarp and a couple of cans of paint. He walked right to the white van, put the supplies in the back, and climbed up into the driver's seat.

It wasn't Eddy.

Had this person borrowed the van from Eddy? No, you could tell from the way he knew exactly where to find the seat belt that this was *his* van. Maybe Eddy had borrowed it from him? Either way, finding that van hadn't brought us any closer to Eddy himself.

It was now after five o'clock. We'd been out in the sun most of the day.

"It doesn't matter," Curtis said calmly, patiently. "We'll come back tomorrow."

At this point, we had no choice.

The next day, Thursday, we did the same thing all over again. We did see another white van, and waited a couple of hours to see the owner, but it wasn't Eddy.

Before we knew it, five o clock had rolled around again. I was blistered and sweaty and headachy and even more sunburned and definitely ready to go home.

"We can't go home," Curtis said.

"Why not?" I said.

"Because that's what we did yesterday. Maybe Eddy is on a schedule of some sort. Maybe he doesn't get home until after five."

"I thought you said he didn't *have* a job," I said.

"Maybe it's not a job," Curtis said. "Maybe he's on a schedule for some other reason. He worked at the diner as a front for a robbery, didn't he? Anyway, we need to keep looking."

"You couldn't have thought of this earlier?" I said.

"Like this morning, before we didn't pack sandwiches or anything else to eat?"

"Suck it up," Curtis said. "It's for a cause bigger than your stomach."

Even I knew that Curtis was right, so we called our parents and told them we had to work late, and kept looking for Eddy, late into the sandwich-less night.

We still didn't find him.

The next day, Friday, we came back, sandwiches in tow. We weren't weirdly animated anymore; after three days of heatstroke, starvation, and aimless wandering, we were all in foul moods. I think we also knew that our one last chance at success with Project Sweet Life was quickly slipping away. I'd told Curtis and Victor about the back-to-school shopping my mother had planned for the following morning, and I think the consequences of our failure were finally seeming real. I was almost ready to suggest we go back to the fortune cookie idea.

We'd started out in the early afternoon. By late afternoon, we'd seen three Eddy-less white vans. But by seven thirty that evening, we still hadn't seen Eddy.

And that's when we ran into him.

Not his van—the man himself.

We were walking down the street. Suddenly a man flew out of the apartment building on our left. He was in a big hurry, pushing right through us. He offered no apology before running off down the street.

"That was Eddy!" I whispered. "We know where he lives!"

"Don't whisper," Curtis said. "Whispering calls attention to itself. People instinctively hear the hushed tones."

I glared at him. "You're just making stuff up again, aren't you?"

"Yeah," he admitted. But at least now he had the decency to look guilty about it.

I changed the topic back to the one at hand. "Now we know where Eddy lives—let's go to the police!"

Victor shook his head. "We don't *know* Eddy lives in this building—maybe he was just visiting a friend. And even if he does live here, so what? We can't call the police and say, 'We think this guy's a bank robber.' No, we need evidence."

239

"Evidence?" I said.

"Something that ties Eddy to the bank robberies," Curtis said. "Victor's right. That's how we're going to get that reward."

"But that would mean getting *inside* his apartment," I whispered, forgetting what Curtis had said about hushed tones. "How are we going to do that?"

No one answered me. We looked over at the apartment building. It was made of brick with small, blocky balconies stacked above the entrance, one for each of the five floors. A pattern of Ionic columns embellished the roofline. It had probably been a grand structure in its day, but that had been a long time ago. Now the bricks were dingy, and the paint on the wooden windowsills and balconies was cracked and peeling.

"We need to do another stakeout," Victor said. "But that means—what is it? Three days? Four? And we'll need delivery uniforms. Something that makes it look like we fit in."

"There's no time!" I said. I reminded them about my mom's back-to-school shopping trip the following morning.

"I still can't believe she's making *you* pay," Curtis said. "That's totally unfair!"

"The point is," I said, "if I don't have the money, my parents are going to know I don't have a job. And then it's only a matter of time before your dads find out too."

"But even if we do implicate Eddy," Victor said, "it's not like we'll get the reward money by tomorrow afternoon."

I nodded. "I know. But it's one thing to be caught in a lie when your lie turned out to be a total disaster. It's another thing to be caught in a lie when the lie ended up catching a bank robber."

We thought about that for second. Then Curtis turned and started up the front steps of Eddy's apartment building.

"Wait!" Victor said. "Where are you going?"

"Inside Eddy's apartment," Curtis said. "There's no time for a stakeout, so we need to do this now."

So Curtis was being his usual, impulsive self. But it wasn't just Curtis. I was edgy and irritable and impatient and totally ready for this endless summer to be over, not to mention still terrified of my parents finding out the truth about Project Sweet Life. If we were going to catch a bank robber by tomorrow afternoon, Curtis was right: We needed to do this now.

"But what about Eddy?" Victor said. "He could be back any second."

"He was in a big hurry," Curtis said. "People in a big hurry are in a hurry to get *to* something. Something important. And important things take time. Besides, it's Friday. I'm sure he's gone for the evening."

Curtis was obviously just making things up again. But I wanted to believe him this time, and I guess Victor did too, because neither of us called him on it.

We followed Curtis up the steps. The doors to the apartment building had been propped open with cinder blocks because of the heat. There was a row of dented metal mailboxes in the foyer just inside.

"Here's an E. Drake," I said, pointing to one of the mailboxes.

"There's also an E. Lannister," Victor said.

"The apartment numbers are listed on the boxes," Curtis said. "So let's check 'em both."

We tried E. Drake's apartment first, which was located on the third floor. The stairs of the building were marble, but deeply indented from a century of footsteps. The hallway carpets were frayed and faded. The whole building smelled of dust and cooking grease.

We stopped in front of E. Drake's apartment. Curtis knocked on the door, and it rattled in its frame.

No one answered. We didn't even hear any movement inside the apartment.

"No one's home," Curtis said. "This must be Eddy's place."

"How do we know?" I said. "Maybe E. Lannister isn't home either."

"Good point," Curtis said.

E. Lannister lived on the fifth floor, but we walked up and knocked on the door of that apartment too. A skinny woman in a red headband answered the door. She looked like she'd been cleaning house.

"Is Eddy here?" Curtis asked.

She stared at us blankly. "Uh, no," she said. "I think you have the wrong apartment."

After she closed the door, Curtis looked at Victor and me. "Well, that's it then. Eddy's last name is Drake, and that was his apartment."

Which meant, of course, that now we had to go break into it!

We returned to the third floor. Curtis walked right up to the door of E. Drake's apartment, facing it like a dance partner.

"Don't tell me," Victor said. "You know how to pick locks?"

"Well," he said, "I've read about it on the internet."

As Curtis stared down the lock on that door, I looked down the hallway. Televisions murmured and electric fans sputtered behind the peeled paint of the other apartment doors. Were people spying on us through the peepholes? Standing there, I felt completely naked and exposed.

"Hurry," I whispered to Curtis.

"Don't whisper," Curtis said.

Curtis picked the lock just like I knew he would. We quickly stepped into that empty apartment and slid the door closed behind us. We kept the lights off. It was already dark outside, but there was just enough of a glow from the streetlights that we could make out the lumpy furniture and the mess.

When it comes to homes, there are two kinds of mess: cluttered-messy and dirty-messy. An apartment can be cluttered and disorganized but not necessarily dirty.

Eddy's apartment was both cluttered *and* dirty. Clothes had been strewn everywhere, and pizza boxes littered the floor. Loose white paper—bills and take-out menus—glowed in the dark. And unlike the woman on the fifth floor, Eddy hadn't been doing any housecleaning lately: Rancid smells floated over from both the kitchen and bathroom areas, and the whole apartment smelled like cigarette smoke.

"Search," Curtis said. "Look for anything that was stolen from Mrs. Shelby's house."

There wasn't anything in the front room. But in the clutter atop the dresser in the bedroom, I saw a glint.

I stepped closer. It was a gold necklace.

A *woman's* gold necklace. I remembered the jewelry I'd seen spilling from the box on Mrs. Shelby's bureau.

"Bingo," I said.

Victor stepped up beside me. He pointed to other

stuff on top of that dresser: a gold watch still in its case, diamond earrings, even a couple of figurines from *The Wizard of Oz*—all stuff we'd seen on Mrs. Shelby's dining room table.

Curtis, Victor, and I looked at one another and smiled. First we'd found Eddy, and now we had some solid evidence that tied him to a crime. Could it be that our luck had finally changed?

But it was at that exact moment that we heard a key being slid into the lock in the front door. Eddy was back.

No, I thought, *our luck hasn't changed!* I also thought, *Why didn't we think to have one of us standing as a lookout out on the stairs?*

"The bathroom!" Curtis whispered.

We all ran for the bathroom. There was no point in hiding in the tub because the shower curtain was clear plastic—grimy, but clear. So we stood just inside the door with the light turned off. Now we just had to hope that the bathroom wasn't the reason Eddy had come home.

We listened to Eddy—the jingling of his keys, his soft sigh, the shuffle of his feet.

We held our breath, desperate to hear where Eddy was going. The bathroom?

No. The bedroom.

This could work, I thought. The bathroom was between the bedroom and the front door. If he stayed in that bedroom, we could make it to the door and out, maybe even without being heard.

We all instinctively seemed to know this. As soon as Eddy had entered the bedroom, we tiptoed out of the bathroom and turned toward the front door.

At that moment, Eddy stepped back out of the bedroom and faced us in the hallway.

"What the—?" he said, confusion in his eyes.

Wow, I thought, *our luck* really *hasn't changed!*

Victor and I both froze as if in a spotlight. But Curtis was right there with a lie on the tip of his tongue.

"I'm sorry," he said to Eddy. "Is this the wrong apartment? We're looking for someone named Lannister."

Eddy hesitated for a fraction of a second. It was a good lie, and Curtis had spoken it with his usual, practiced innocence. But Victor and I must have looked too frightened, our faces too flushed, and Eddy was no fool.

"How'd you get in here?" he said. "That door was locked. Wait, you were already in here when I got home, weren't you? How'd you get in? What did you see? What do you *want*?" For the record, there was no confusion in his eyes anymore. It was scary how quickly he was piecing things together. He was a thief and a slob, but not stupid.

"Nothing," Curtis said, his voice catching at last. "I told you we were looking for Mrs. Lannister."

"You're lying," Eddy said, but he wasn't rude about it. "Let's talk. I can make it worth your while."

He took a step toward us so he was barely five feet away.

Victor and I froze again.

But Curtis said, *"Run!"*

We lunged toward the front door. Fortunately, Curtis brought up the rear, so when Eddy grabbed him from behind, he somehow managed to wiggle free just as I threw open the door.

We ran—through the doorway and down the dusty hallway, down the deeply grooved marble stairs and out into the street.

Eddy followed. But he was an old guy, and we were three fit fifteen-year-olds. Besides, what exactly could he do even if he did catch us?

Outside the apartment building, I glanced back. Eddy was barely ten feet behind us. On the plus side, we really were faster than he was; he seemed to be losing ground.

Then I saw the gun in his hand.

"I'd call the police on my cell phone!" Victor said, even as we kept sprinting down the street. "Except—wait! I sold it eight weeks ago in our garage sale!"

"You are not seriously *still* going on about that!" Curtis said.

He can't shoot us, I thought. *It's downtown. People would see. There'd be witnesses.*

But the truth was, it was after eight now, and the streets were deserted. Downtown Tacoma had gentrified, but not yet to the point that it had any kind of nightlife. And when I looked behind us again, I saw that Eddy had somehow slipped a black ski mask on over his head.

Now he's wearing a mask? I thought. *Where had that come from?* Or was a mask just something that a thief always carried with him—like a pocketknife or breath mints for most people?

"I have a plan!" Curtis said suddenly, even as we all kept running.

Curtis had a plan! I wasn't sure whether to be relieved or even more terrified.

We kept running downhill and reached the Spanish Steps—those white stairs that led down into the Old City Hall District. That's when I realized where Curtis was taking us.

"You are *not* seriously thinking of leading him down there!" I said.

"Why not?" Curtis said. "It's perfect!"

Then the second part of Curtis's plan occurred to me. And I immediately thought to myself, *What the heck, this just might work!*

When we came to Fireman's Park, I could still hear Eddy's footsteps thundering behind us. I looked back and saw we'd gained about forty feet on him.

We found the clump of ground cover with the metal grate that led down to the China Tunnels. We threw the grate to one side, but as we crouched to crawl down the shaft, the footsteps behind us stopped.

I looked up. Eddy had stopped running and was aiming his gun right at us.

"Saint Asparagus!" Victor said. For once, his invented saint made no sense whatsoever. But under the circumstances, I couldn't really blame him.

Eddy fired.

My eyes bulged as I stood there expecting to feel hot metal sizzling through my flesh. In the nearby greenbelt, I heard the panicked scatter of feral cats.

But I didn't feel anything. The report of the gunshot echoed. Eddy had missed. When I looked at my friends, I saw them both scurrying for the rungs of the metal ladder that vanished in the darkness.

Eddy fired again, but this time I didn't wait to see if I'd been hit. I scrambled after Curtis and Victor into the shadows of the China Tunnels.

Would Eddy follow us? Even before my feet touched the ground at the bottom of that ladder, I knew he would. Sure enough, the rungs of the ladder squeaked and wrenched above us.

That's when I also realized the flaw in Curtis's plan: If Curtis's plan *didn't* work, Eddy was free to kill us in complete privacy, and no one would ever know what had happened. What if he had a flashlight along with the gun and ski mask in his pockets? We had no light whatsoever, which meant that Curtis's plan would be over before it had even begun.

"This way!" Curtis said, heading off into the darkness, and I knew that he'd spoken as much for Eddy's benefit as for Victor and me. The whole point was to get Eddy to follow us.

But it was dark, and the tunnels were anything but straight. What if Curtis couldn't find what he was looking for? What if we ran right into a loose spike or nail, or hit our heads on a low-hanging beam?

We fumbled forward, feeling our way rather than seeing it. The scuffles and muttered curse words that echoed in back of us told me that Eddy was right behind.

"Stop!" Curtis whispered suddenly, blocking Victor and me with his outstretched arms. "We're here."

We had reached the abandoned subterranean prison under Old City Hall. But I knew it wasn't the old cells that Curtis was planning on trapping Eddy in; it was that open sinkhole in the middle of the floor *outside* the cells. I could somehow *feel* the open pit right in front of us. That said, I hadn't sensed it until just then, which meant we had almost walked right into it.

Would Eddy sense it too?

Quietly, Curtis prodded us over toward the cells, where we could wait to see if our web was going to catch this fly.

But behind us in the hallway, I saw something I definitely didn't want to see.

Light. Something was flickering in the near-total blackness.

Eddy had a lighter! How could we have forgotten that Eddy was a smoker?

This was bad. With a source of light, Eddy was sure to see the hole in the ground. He was also likely to see *us*! We'd cornered ourselves in the cells. If we tried to go forward, Eddy would hear us for sure.

Slowly, Eddy inched closer. He must have heard that we'd stopped moving, that we were waiting for him, and while he may or may not have sensed the open pit, he had to know something was up.

A globe of flickering light entered the prison chamber. In the amber glow of the flame, Eddy's face looked cadaverous—his eyes dark and hollowed, his skin haggard. But at least he hadn't yet spotted the hole in the floor.

"Don't shoot," Curtis said suddenly. "We're in here."

Curtis! I wanted to say. *What are you doing?!*

Eddy's face crumpled into a big smile. But to get a clear shot at us, he had to step forward into the middle of the room, right toward the pit.

Now I saw why Curtis had spoken. He assumed Eddy would see the pit with his light, so he'd drawn his attention toward us, up off the floor.

"We'll talk," Curtis said. "Just don't shoot us."

"Talk?" Eddy said, strolling calmly forward. "What's to talk about?"

And that's when he stepped right into the open pit.

The lighter snuffed out the second he began to fall. He screamed as he plummeted downward.

We heard him hit the floor with a painful thump. He groaned softly, so we knew he was still conscious.

"Let's get out of here," Curtis said.

Eddy fired his gun up at us, again and again. Unlike the flickering lighter, the orange flashes brightly illuminated the whole prison. But now because of the angle, he didn't have a shot at us.

But in those flashes of gunfire, I saw something under our feet in that cell.

It was those pieces of crushed plaster of Paris and drops of paint we'd seen before, the ones we'd thought had something to do with the gamers from the Dungeon Door. Something about the mess nagged at me.

We didn't want to give Eddy a chance to shoot out a brick over our heads, so we hurried away, leaving him in the sinkhole.

"We did it," Victor said once we were safe. "We got him! Let's go call the police. We'll tell them everything."

But something about that plaster of Paris and those little drops of paint still bugged me.

Then suddenly I had it. Could the answer to Project Sweet Life have been with us all along? It seemed too incredible to be true. Maybe I was jumping to conclusions again. But the more I thought about it, the more convinced I became that it *was* true. It was like the whole summer was coming into focus, almost like everything we'd done had been for a reason.

Curtis, Victor, and I climbed out of the China Tunnels. We called the police from a pay phone on the street near Old City Hall. I did the talking. I told them about Eddy— how he'd been involved in the Capitol American bank robberies, how he'd also broken into Mrs. Shelby's house, and how he was currently trapped in a sinkhole under the streets of downtown Tacoma. I was very specific about everything, including Eddy's address and the fact that he currently had lots of stolen loot inside his apartment. But I didn't give them our names.

Then I hung up the phone.

"What are you doing?" Curtis said. "You didn't tell them about us. That we were the ones who caught him."

"I know," I said.

"But the reward!"

"We don't *need* that reward," I said. "We already have more money than we could possibly spend—more than enough for Project Sweet Life and then some."

"Tell me more," Curtis said.

I smiled. I would tell them everything. But not just yet.

WEEK 10:

The Sweet Life

First, we watched from near the Spanish Steps to make sure the police had believed me about a guy trapped in the tunnels under downtown Tacoma. A few minutes later, three cars arrived. The officers went right to where I had said the entrance to the tunnels would be. Would the police have enough evidence to get a warrant to search Eddy's apartment in order to find the stolen loot? Maybe there had been some witnesses to Eddy chasing us down the streets of downtown Tacoma and shooting at us. At this point, that was now between Eddy and the police.

I turned toward our bikes, parked several blocks away. "Let's go," I said.

"We're really leaving?" Curtis said. "We're really not going to talk to the police?"

"We're really not going to talk to the police," I said calmly.

"But why?" Victor said.

"I can't just tell you," I said. "I have to show you. It's the only way to prove I'm right."

"You *better* be right," Curtis said. "Because we're giving up a hundred-thousand-dollar reward!"

That's when I realized how cool the air was. At some point in the last few hours, the heat wave had broken.

"I'm right," I said. "I'm absolutely positive."

It was almost eleven before we made it back to Curtis's. I'd called my parents from the road and asked if I could spend the night at the bomb shelter. They'd said yes, so we still had the whole night ahead of us.

"Okay, okay!" Curtis said once we were inside the seclusion of our hideout. "What's this all about?"

"I know what happened to the Labash coins," I said.

"We *all* know what happened to the Labash coins,"

Victor said. "They were hidden in the China Tunnels, but the owners of the Dungeon Door found them, framed them, and hung them on their basement wall."

"No," I said. "I don't know what those coins hanging on the wall were—props from *The Pirates of the Caribbean* movie maybe? But I know they weren't the Labash coins. Because the Labash coins have been with us all along."

Curtis's eyes met mine. I think he thought I was joking or possibly crazy—that the pressure of Project Sweet Life and the threat of losing my two best friends had caused my mind to snap.

"I'm not crazy," I said, "and I'll prove it."

I picked up our statue of Mr. Moneybags from the floor. I lifted it up as if to smash it against the ground.

"Dave?" Victor said. "What do you think you're doing?"

"Yeah!" Curtis said. "That's our mascot!"

"Trust me," I said.

I hurled the statue to the concrete floor of the bomb shelter with all my might.

It hadn't broken when it hit the Ferrari all those weeks ago, but I threw it hard, and this time it shattered—

though with a dull thud, not a sharp crash. I bent down and started rifling through the pieces.

The statue wasn't ceramic. It was plaster of Paris painted with enamel. The remnants looked and smelled like crushed chalk. As I rooted through them, the pieces crumbled into white powder.

And almost right away, I found what I was looking for.

I held a gold coin in my hand.

I placed it on the floor and kept combing through the powder. I quickly found three more coins.

"What are . . . ?" Curtis started to say.

"They're the gold coins that Mr. Haft stole from Mr. Labash," I said.

"Holy Perplexica," Victor said, "patron saint of the totally confused!"

Meanwhile, Curtis's eyes bugged. "But how did they get *inside* Mr. Moneybags?"

"They've been there all along. That's where Mr. Haft hid them, not down in the China Tunnels where we thought."

This was all coming too fast. Curtis and Victor didn't

understand. "Wait," Victor said. "Go back. Start at the beginning. Tell me how all this fits together."

I took a breath. "Ron Haft stole the Labash coins from that downtown coin shop and used the China Tunnels to make his escape. But he didn't hide the coins down there like I thought. Maybe he knew that other people were using the tunnels too, and he worried that they might find the coins. Or maybe he just didn't want to let his precious coins out of his sight. He was worried he might be a suspect in the theft, so he needed a really good place to hide the coins, at least until everything blew over. He decided to hide them in plain sight—inside an object at his office that everyone there would have been familiar with."

"Mr. Moneybags!" Victor said. "Mr. Haft had a sense of humor."

"But how in the world did he get the money *inside* a statue?" Curtis said.

"He didn't," I said. "The first statue, the one that had been in his office, was made of porcelain. But he used the original to make a duplicate out of plaster of Paris." I stepped on one of the pieces of the statue at my feet; it crushed into powder under my heel. "Then after it dried, he painted the plaster with enamel paint to make it look like the original."

"Down in the China Tunnels!" Victor said suddenly. "That's where he did it. We saw the leftover plaster and the spattered paint."

I nodded. "But once he had the new statue, he needed to get rid of the old one so it wouldn't look suspicious."

"We saw that too!" Curtis said. "In the water down by the ruins of the Chinese settlement."

I nodded again. "He couldn't just throw the original Mr. Moneybags away, because he knew the police might go through his garbage. So Mr. Haft took the original statue and carried it through the China Tunnels to that exit just above where Chinatown used to be. Then he walked down to the water near the site of that old settlement and tossed the statue into the bay, thinking that no one would ever find it. And no one ever *would* have found it, if it hadn't been made of porcelain, which meant barnacles wouldn't grow on it."

"But what an amazing coincidence!" Curtis said. "We were trying to find the hidden Labash coins down in the China Tunnels, and we just happen to *own* the very thing that they're hidden inside?"

"It wasn't a coincidence at all," I said. "The only reason we started looking for the China Tunnels was because I read about them in *Trains and Totem Poles*, the book you bought at the same estate sale where you also bought that statue of Mr. Moneybags. But I'm pretty sure that wasn't just *any* estate sale. It was the estate sale of Ron Haft. Curtis, don't you remember how you overheard someone saying it was the estate of some local government bigwig? In other words, we learned about the China Tunnels from the same place Mr. Haft did. But it wasn't until I saw the leftover plaster of Paris in that abandoned dungeon that I finally put all the pieces together."

Curtis and Victor were speechless. Frankly, I'd surprised myself a little too. I'm not stupid, but I don't consider myself brilliant either. I guess everyone gets lucky sometimes.

"Dave!" Curtis said. "That's fantastic! I can't believe you figured that all out!"

I shrugged matter-of-factly. "Piece-o-cake," I said.

There were forty-two gold coins in all. But we didn't want to get too excited until we were absolutely sure that the coins were ours to keep. After all, Mr. Haft had stolen them from Mr. Labash. True, Mr. Labash had turned out to be pretty evil, murdering Mr. Haft and all. But what if he had a business partner, or some other relative? We didn't want to do to them what Mrs. Shelby had done to us.

Still, I did take one of those forty-two coins. I figured I'd earned it. And the next day, when my mom took me back-to-school shopping at the mall, I encouraged her to stop at J.C. Penney first to try on some shoes for herself. As she did, I slipped over to the coin shop at the mall and asked what they'd give me for the coin.

"Five hundred dollars," the guy said quickly, trying hard not to appear too eager.

I'd looked up the coin's real value online that morning, and this was way under. I also got the feeling that he wasn't supposed to be dealing with anyone under eighteen. But with my mom waiting for me nine stores away, I was in no position to bargain. So I took the cash, which was more than enough to pay for my back-to-school shopping.

Only one more lie, I told myself. But it was funny, because the closer we came to the end of summer, each new lie was becoming more difficult to tell.

"Ready?" my mom said when I found her in J.C. Penney.

"Ready," I said. And I *was* ready, not just for shopping, but for this whole summer of lies to finally be over.

But there were still a few more lies to be told. We couldn't let our parents know about the Labash coins, or they'd learn about Project Sweet Life too. That said, we did need an adult to find out if we owned the coins fair and square and, if so, to sell them for us. So on Sunday we made another visit to Uncle Brad and Uncle Danny.

We sat in the front room of their house and explained everything.

"Oh, come on," Uncle Brad said when I was finished. "Are you sure you didn't let your imaginations get away from you?"

So we showed them *Trains and Totem Poles*, and the coins, and the online printouts of what we'd learned they were worth.

A smile tugged at the corner of Uncle Danny's mouth. "I think they really did it," he said to Uncle Brad, who had also begun to smirk.

They started laughing.

"You did it!" Uncle Brad said. "You really did it!"

They'd laughed at us once before, when we'd first told them about Project Sweet Life. But this was a different kind of laughter. This time they weren't laughing *at* us, but *with* us.

It was funny how up until then I hadn't let myself get excited. I guess it was the fact that we'd gotten ahead of ourselves so many times over the course of the summer, and it had always led to some big disappointment. Plus, there was the whole lying-to-my-parents thing, which I still felt bad about.

But for the first time since the summer began, we'd actually gotten something right. That was finally sinking in.

Before I knew it, we were all slapping each other on the backs and laughing so hard that our sides ached.

By Wednesday of that last week in August, Uncle Brad and Uncle Danny had talked to a lawyer about claims of ownership on the Labash coins.

"Calvin Labash had no living relatives and no will," Uncle Brad explained. "By being convicted of homicide and then killing himself, his estate lost any claim to the coins. Meanwhile, Ron Haft died deeply in debt. This explains why it took them so long to hold his estate sale—it's been held in escrow all this time while his creditors battled it out. But a court finally ruled that all his possessions be sold as is."

"What does that mean for the coins?" I said. "Are they really ours?"

Uncle Brad nodded. "Legally, you bought them fair and square when you bought Mr. Moneybags at the estate sale for two dollars."

The next day, Uncle Brad sold the first of the coins to a shop in Seattle.

For eleven thousand dollars.

It was more than enough to prove to our fathers that we'd had summer jobs. We could also pay back the money we owed to Uncle Brad and Uncle Danny for repairing the neighbor's Ferrari.

The estimated value of all the coins together was 1.6 million dollars.

"Holy Saint Powerball!" Victor said when we found out the total. "We're *rich!*"

School would start on Tuesday of the following

week. That meant we had four whole days of complete freedom to do whatever we wanted before the end of summer.

But the lying still wasn't over. After all, Fircrest Pool stayed open through Labor Day, so I had to continue going to "work." I decided to take Labor Day off—one fewer day of lies—so Sunday was my last official day as a fake lifeguard.

That Monday, the last day of summer vacation, my dad told me over dinner that he'd stopped by my workplace earlier that day.

I almost choked on my chicken-nugget salad.

"What?" I said.

"Oh, I know you said that your manager didn't want family members bothering you at work," he said. "But this was different. I didn't want to talk to you; I wanted to talk to *him*. So I walked right in and said, 'I'm Dave's dad, and I want to know exactly how he did working for you this summer.'"

"Dad, I can explain!" I said.

"You can?"

"Yes!" But could I? I could explain about the stolen

Labash coins. But could I explain about lying to my parents? Was there anything I could say that would make *that* make sense?

The only thing I could do was try.

I told my parents the whole story of the summer from start to finish. I even told them about the coins and their being worth 1.6 million dollars.

Two minutes into the story, my mom dropped her fork onto her plate with a clunk.

Three minutes in, my dad's face started to get very red.

But I kept talking, and they listened to it all. In a way, it was a relief to finally have it all out in the open. No more lies.

When I was done, no one said anything.

"Don't just sit there," I said. "Say something."

My dad's face was so red now that, for a second, I worried he was choking.

But then he sighed, deeper than I'd ever heard him sigh. "Dave, Dave, Dave," he said at last.

"Well," my mom said sadly, "this explains why you never complained about your job and never left wet towels on the bathroom floor."

In other words, I thought, *I'm a complete disappointment to you both*. Didn't the fact that my friends and I had made 1.6 million dollars mean *anything*? It was like they'd completely missed that part.

"For the record," my dad said, "would you like to know what the manager at the Fircrest Pool said to me?"

"Sure," I said meekly. "What?"

"He said that Dave has been an excellent employee and that he'd definitely be welcome back at the pool next summer."

Huh? I thought. Then I realized: *There was someone else named Dave working at the Fircrest Pool!*

Which meant I'd just confessed Project Sweet Life to my parents for no reason whatsoever. I'd made it past my dad's keenly tuned "surveyor's sense" all summer long—only to get caught by my own mistake. Could I really have been so careless? I wasn't just a complete disappointment to my parents; I was also a total idiot. And now Curtis, Victor, and I were all going to pay the price.

"It wasn't fair," I mumbled.

"What wasn't fair?" my dad said.

"Your making me get a summer job," I said, louder.

"I'm only fifteen years old." *I might as well say what I'm thinking, I thought. At this point, how can I make things worse?*

"And there's some kind of unwritten rule that a fifteen-year-old can't get a summer job?" my dad said.

"He *can* get a summer job," I said, "but he isn't *required* to *That's* the unwritten rule! Everyone knows that. Your making me get a summer job, that wasn't fair."

"So that gives you the right to lie to me?"

"Yes!" I said. But then I said, "No. I mean, okay, it was wrong of me to lie to you. But it was wrong of you too, to make me spend my last summer of freedom doing something I didn't want to do. You didn't even listen when I tried to explain!"

My dad looked at my mom. I looked at her too. But she was smart enough not to say anything, to just sit there sipping her cranberry-papaya juice blend.

My dad banged his fist on the table. *"Enough!"* he said to me. "You and your friends have been lying all summer long! And if you think you can somehow blame me for that, you are sadly mistaken. And if you think you're going to keep spending time with those two juvenile delinquents, you're mistaken about that too. *You are who you surround yourself with!"*

So here at last was the anger I'd expected, and the punishment too. Like I said, my dad likes things in black-and-white. But how was I going to live without Curtis and Victor as my friends?

Then I had a realization. Unlike the secret of the Labash coins, it was something so straightforward and obvious I couldn't believe I hadn't thought of it before.

"No," I said to my dad.

"No?" my dad said, his face reddening again. "No, *what?"*

"No, I'm *not* who I surround myself with," I said. "I'm not sure that was true even when I was a kid. But I'm not a kid anymore, and it's definitely not true now. I'm *more* than the people around me. I'm my own person. We all are."

My dad started to speak, but my mom spoke up at last, cutting him off. "No. Let Dave finish."

So I finished. "And even if it is true?" I said. "I don't think I could surround myself with anyone better than Curtis and Victor."

"Those con artists?" my dad said, his face now valentine

red. "Those *liars*? How could they *possibly* be a good influence?"

So I explained how when we'd been captured by the bank robbers, my two friends had both been so quick to offer their lives for me. I explained how when we'd broken into Mrs. Shelby's house, it hadn't been to steal from her but to prove once and for all that we *didn't* steal. And I explained how once we'd started looking for Lei-Lei Tang's hidden treasure, we'd all agreed to donate most of it to the Chinese Reconciliation Project. The more I thought about it, the more I remembered a million other examples of how much integrity Victor and, in his own way, even Curtis had: the way Victor had always insisted that everything about Project Sweet Life be perfectly legal or the way Curtis had treated those women at the Evergreen Assisted Living Center.

"You can punish me for what I did this summer," I said to my dad. "I accept that. But you can't take away my friendship with Curtis and Victor. Because the person who decides who I surround myself with now is me, not you. And personally, I can't imagine surrounding myself with anyone better than them."

When I was finished, my dad just stared at me, eyes bulging. I had struck him speechless again.

Still, I noticed his face wasn't quite as red as before.

I'd like to say my brilliant speech to my parents meant I didn't get punished.

I'd like to say that, but it isn't true. I did get punished. When my dad told Curtis's and Victor's dads, they got punished too. Interestingly, we all got the same punishment (clearly, our dads talked).

First, we lost our allowances for good. Given that our net worth now exceeded our parents', this was only fair.

Next, we all had to put most of our individual shares of the money aside to pay taxes and as investments for college. (But—duh!—we would have done that anyway. We also had to give a pretty big donation to the Reconciliation Project, but again, this was something we were planning on doing anyway.)

Finally, our parents made us agree to do volunteer work every Saturday until Christmas break. We suggested the same organization that Haleigh and Lani had volunteered with, which meant we could go back and see the women at the Evergreen Assisted Living Center.

But my dad never said anything more about my not being friends with Curtis and Victor. And so far, I've never again heard him use that expression about how we are who we surround ourselves with.

So did my friends and I find the sweet life? Given the fact that we ended up with more than a million dollars, it's hard to argue otherwise. But the whole point of Project Sweet Life was to create one last completely work-free *summer*—one last drink at the oasis of freedom before heading off through the harsh desert of a lifetime of employment. In the end, we'd spent the summer working a lot harder than if we'd just gotten jobs to begin with, with a lot more frustration and disappointment too. Just the other day, Curtis, Victor, and I were talking about the irony.

"Think about all we did this summer," Curtis said. "I mean, it's kind of incredible."

It was mid-October, not even two months since Labor Day, and the three of us were sitting in the whirlpool we'd had installed in Curtis's backyard, right next to the bomb shelter. With some of the money from the coin sale, we'd also replaced most of what we'd sold at the beginning of the summer. Our new television, for example, was an 82-inch LCD flat-panel television with a high-end audio system. And the same contractor who'd put in the whirlpool had also built us our own bathroom and shower.

"Our summer wasn't exactly lying around the pool drinking lemonade, that's for sure," Victor said.

"Yeah," Curtis said, "but it was some pretty interesting stuff. In the end, we did all the things we'd planned on doing—scuba diving, bike riding, even spelunking of sorts—plus a whole bunch of other stuff we never would've done in a million years."

Curtis had a point. I hadn't really thought about the summer quite that way before.

"Sure, we got frustrated or annoyed at times," he went on. "But didn't that just push us to be smarter and more creative?"

"I wouldn't have minded a little less pushing and a little more lemonade," Victor said.

Curtis and I laughed. But at the same time, I was reminded how the summer had made me feel so much closer to my two friends. In a way, I even felt closer to my parents. Would any of that have happened if we hadn't had to work so hard?

The warm water felt good bubbling against my skin. I leaned back in the whirlpool, and I couldn't help but think more about what Curtis had said. Yes, we'd worked hard over the summer, but we'd had fun, too, and it was all very satisfying in the long run. Why? Well, because we did things entirely on our own terms. And honestly, how could life get any sweeter than that?

Then again, I thought as I soaked in the warm water, there was also definitely something to be said for LCD televisions and backyard whirlpools.

AUTHOR'S NOTE

The historical events described in my book concerning the expulsion of the Chinese from the city of Tacoma are fictionalized but are based on historical fact.

In the 1870s, two-thirds of the workers who built the Western Division of America's Northern Pacific Railroad were Chinese. In the 1880s, after the completion of the rail line, many settled on the West Coast, including in Tacoma, working as waiters, servants, launderers, and garbage collectors. But the economy turned sour. Many people, especially the unions, blamed the Chinese for being willing to work for low wages; in reality, the

Chinese were merely trying to survive, and no American labor union had ever invited them to join their movement and organize for better working conditions.

The anti-Chinese sentiment was particularly nasty in Tacoma, which blamed many of its problems on its Chinese population. Tacoma mayor Jacob Robert Weisbach (himself a recent immigrant, from Germany) referred to the Chinese as a "filthy horde." Jack Comerford, the editor of the *Tacoma Ledger*, wrote racist diatribes in his newspaper. Local unions held angry meetings. The few dissenters who urged tolerance were ignored.

In 1885, the city gave its Chinese residents a deadline: Leave town by November third. One Chinese man, Goon Gau, wired the territorial governor for help and protection, saying he feared the angry mob. He was ignored.

Some Chinese had left town early, but more than half, about two hundred people, remained behind on November third. A crowd of white people, including the mayor and city officials, descended on the part of town where the Chinese lived. They pulled guns, broke doors and windows, and rounded up all the residents, marching them to the rail station and forcing them on the morning train to Portland, Oregon. Later, the mob burned the houses and pushed the wreckage into the water of Commencement Bay. Most of the Chinese lost everything and never returned to Tacoma. Some of the perpetrators were indicted, but the judge let them free on bail; Tacoma celebrated with a parade. Later, all charges against them were dropped. The "Tacoma Method" for dealing with immigrants became famous and was even considered by other cities.

To this day, unlike its neighbors to the north and south, Tacoma has no Chinatown.

In 1993, the Tacoma City Council finally passed a resolution apologizing for the actions of the city and its leaders. A citizens' committee was created, which led to the creation of a Chinese Reconciliation Project. The project includes a commemorative park not far from the site of Tacoma's original Chinese settlement.

ACKNOWLEDGMENTS

If the sweet life really is, in part, about the people you surround yourself with, my life is sweet indeed. The important people in my life who contributed to this book include Michael Jensen, my partner since 1992; Ruth Katcher, my editor; Jennifer DeChiara, my agent; Elyse Marshall, Dina Sherman, Patty Rosati, Lillie Walsh, and all the other terrific folks at HarperCollins; and Tom Baer, Tim Cathersal, John Dempsey, Steve Gernon, and Scott Jarmon, with whom I shared plenty of teenage adventures of my own, some of which were just as crazy as the ones described here (and some of which *were* the ones described here!).

Special thanks to Anjali Banerjee for thoughtful feedback; to Dave Meconi and Laura Hanan for generously granting me access to their downtown Tacoma basements; and to Bill Middlebrook, who shared with me the details of his underwater exploration of the wreckage of Tacoma's original Chinese settlement.

Finally, thanks to the city of Tacoma, my hometown. As a boy, you disappointed me more times than I can count. But I kept believing in you, even before you believed in yourself. And what do you know? After all these years, you're finally starting to get it right.